Woodward Avenue
Part II: Ground Pounders

By Keith MacDonald

Woodward Avenue Part II: Ground Pounders

By Keith MacDonald © 2015
ISBN 978-1-329-67643-5
All Rights Reserved

Printed in the United States of America

Cover design by James Aiello

I am proud of the *Woodward Avenue* series of novels and welcome your comments and/or suggestions at keith@AmericanCarClassics.net

Dedication:
This novel is dedicated to all who have believed in and enjoyed the original "Woodward Avenue" novel and encouraged me, year after year, to write the sequel. Well here it is. I hope you are as satisfied and thrilled as I am. After all, "It's all about Woodward."

The US Department of Transportation has named Woodward Avenue the Automotive Heritage Trail. It has been named an All-American Road by another agency, a Pure Michigan Byway by the Michigan DOT, and lastly it was included in a late 1990s congressional bill as part of the Motor Cities National Heritage Area. In short, this road is more than just another means to get somewhere and the love and appreciation people have for it will be on full display throughout the summers for decades to come.

–Brian Lohnes
BangShift.com

Out on Woodward, the strokes are roaring up and down, screeching their tires, and every once in a while the fuzz will snap on their gumball revolving lights and pull some guy over and lay maybe a $200 fine on him. This is really a very good deal for the fuzz in Royal Oak and those other suburban towns, because the city fathers can make a lot of bucks off the racers in a given evening. Oh, they talk about the *menace of the street racers*, but they never make any real push to shut down the action. After all, if you can make a few grand in fines every night why spoil a good thing?

Brock Yates
Street Racing

PRELUDE

From *Woodward Avenue*: Montrose, Michigan 1970

Now, where were we?

The strip was brimming with shining steel chariots as night had fallen over northern Detroit. From stoplight to stoplight, well-tuned machines engaged each other in countless duels. The air seemed electrified by the evening's approaching big event.

From outside the parking lot came a thunderous roar, which interrupted Kent Rager's conversation with his mechanic, Quentin. All eyes turned to see what the commotion was about. Tucker Knox's '65 GTO was blocked by several parked cars, but like a grand unveiling, it appeared rounding the entrance to the lot. The car's bellow was earth shaking.

Tucker moved the GTO slowly past Rager and pointed a menacing finger.

"This ends tonight, Rager."

Rager placed his hands on his hips, "Not by a long shot, Nancy."

Tucker pulled the GTO to the other end of the lot as Dawn Holt and Will Hoyt arrived in Dawn's '66 Galaxie 500.

Rager approached the GTO as Tucker exited the vehicle. With a long gaze, Rager took in the lines of the fine looking Pontiac.

"That's a damn fine piece of machinery. It's wasted on a squid like you though. What have you got under there?"

"A whole lot of bad news for you, Rager," returned Tucker.

4

Rager tried his best to unsettle Tucker, "That looks like more muscle than a shit stink like you can handle. Too bad it's a Pontiac. Did you buy this heap with your *Vietnam victim's pay*? What a waste of hard-earned, blood money."

Rager watched for Tucker's reaction, but none was forthcoming. Tucker glowered back at Rager with a steely glare. Rager swallowed hard as he glanced back at his 429, "How 'bout we put pink slips on the line?"

Tucker wasn't going to be intimidated, "I wouldn't have it any other way."

Rager spat on the ground. "You're stupider than you look."

"Fate awaits then," Tucker motioned toward the street.

Rager was noticeably irritated with the way things were going and decided that enough was enough.

"You know the place."

Rager headed back to his Mustang as the crowd excitedly dashed for their vehicles. With a crescendo of engine noise, the convoy began to move out and onto Woodward Avenue.

The fringe of a rundown industrial area was a region devoid of life. Save for a few dancing moths, nothing was moving as the dull street illumination threw ghostly shadows across the asphalt.

With an orgasm of sound, dozens of cars of all shapes and sizes descended upon the area. There were muscle cars, hot rods, sports cars, compacts, family sedans and wagons. They split and found parking on either side of the road.

Kent Rager's Boss 429 Mustang and Tucker's GTO were the last vehicles to arrive and slowly made their way to a yellow stripe painted across the roadway. The crowd emerged from their cars and took up positions using any vantage point available.

Hoyt and Dawn pushed through the throng and stepped into the clearing.

Tucker and Rager exited their vehicles and approached each other, "Okay, this is for pink slips, right?" sneered Rager.

Tucker nodded.

Rager threw Quentin a flashlight, "Let's do this."

Rager and Tucker climbed back into their respective vehicles and fired up the engines. The combined thunder of raw horsepower was no less than spine tingling.
Hoyt and Dawn made their way to the driver's side of the GTO.

"Good luck, man," said Hoyt, "Blow this son-of-a-bitch away."

Dawn leaned into the vehicle and kissed Tucker passionately before whispering, "Be careful, Tuck."

Tucker was taken aback by Dawn's aggressive kiss and watched as she joined the mass of spectators with Hoyt.
Rager revved the Boss Mustang and performed a spectacular burnout. The rear tires spewed clouds of tire smoke into the night sky. Tucker was not going to be outdone and gave the GTO plenty of RPMs. He dropped the clutch, spinning the rear wheels furiously. Blue smoke surged off the fat rubber as the GTO slowly fishtailed away from the line. Both vehicles slowly reversed back onto the yellow start line.

Quentin took his position between the two cars and readied himself. Rager gave the Mustang a hard rev, which motivated Tucker to unleash a thunderous reply from the big Pontiac engine.
Quentin held up the light and switched it on. Both vehicles were given plenty off the mark as they slalomed away from the line. The Mustang was a nose in front as both drivers simultaneously slammed second. Tucker's change was smooth, giving the GTO maximum power as it accelerated through second gear.
Tucker glanced across to see his vehicle pull even with the Mustang.
Rager made a precise third gear change. The monster Ford laid some more rubber and really started to move out. Tucker made a

brilliant third gear change, the GTO responding with a brutish display of acceleration. The GTO's three carburetors worked in tandem as all available torque was transferred to the ground, propelling the GTO at a terrifying rate. Tucker's head was pinned to the headrest, which Hoyt had knowingly installed on the driver's seat. The GTO began to pull away from the Mustang as the finish line loomed ahead.

Knowing defeat was imminent; Rager slammed his fist on the steering wheel.

"No! No! No!"

Tucker punched the air as his GTO streaked across the finish line a car length ahead of Rager's Mustang. The crowd fell silent as they realized that *the king*, Kent Rager had lost the race.

Hoyt and Dawn jumped with sheer delight, embracing each other wildly.

Tucker slowed the vehicle and made a U-turn. He cruised past Rager's Mustang and gave him a wink before returning his victorious GTO to the starting line. As Tucker climbed from the vehicle, he was greeted with much cheering and a very enthusiastic Hoyt and Dawn. The trio embraced.

"Oh, man," spluttered Hoyt, "I knew you could do it."

Tucker was charged with adrenalin, "Hoyt, this car is just so sweet. It was easy, man. I even had horsepower in reserve. What a ball-tearer."

Dawn grabbed Tucker and planted a kiss on his lips, "I think I love you."

Tucker looked dazed by the bold statement.

Hoyt interrupted, "What the hell is he doing?"

Tucker and Dawn looked back up the quarter mile to see the Mustang idling menacingly.

Rager was fuming. His eyes had glazed over as he tightly gripped the steering wheel. His breathing was heavy and it appeared he had lost any semblance of rational thought. Rager slammed the Mustang into first and dropped the clutch.

The crowd watched, completely dumbfounded as the Mustang lit up the rear tires and accelerated toward them. Some began to run for cover. Like a deer in headlights, Tucker watched as the Mustang increased speed and closed in on them.

Rager slammed third gear and jammed his foot on the accelerator. He screamed like a man possessed, as he was now dangerously close. At the last moment, Tucker grabbed Dawn and dove for cover. Hoyt was not far behind them.

Suddenly, three shots were fired from a .357 revolver.

One of the slugs slammed into the front tire of Rager's Mustang. Tucker, Dawn and Hoyt reacted to the gunfire and looked up just in time to see the Mustang swerve dramatically, clip the rear end of the GTO and slide into a ditch. The impact sent the GTO spinning wildly and the Mustang into a violent barrel roll. Sparks and glass flew as the now demolished Mustang brutally bounced across the asphalt before slamming into a wall. The sudden impact caused a massive explosion - killing Rager instantly.

Harlan Boggs was standing alongside his police cruiser as he absorbed the devastation before him. He holstered his revolver and approached the group. Tucker, Hoyt and Dawn were stunned into silence as they tried to soak in the scene before them. Dawn held Tucker close as he just stared at his severely dented GTO.

"Is everyone okay?" asked Boggs.

"Yeah, thanks," replied Tucker.

The burning Mustang exploded again sending a fireball mushrooming into the night sky.

CHAPTER 1

Montrose Memorial Hospital, Michigan 1970

Harlan Boggs looked worn and ragged. He shook his head in disgust as he examined a clipboard, then glanced over at the sheet-covered gurney, shrouding a lifeless shell, which was once the chiseled body of an arrogant and repugnant Kent Rager. Boggs marveled at how these peaceful remains were once filled with such an intense, fiery rage.

"Rager," he huffed. "How appropriate."

A nurse approached him and Boggs signed the clipboard before handing it over to her.

"Will you be notifying next of kin?" Boggs asked.

The nurse shrugged as she gave Boggs a worried glance. "There's no phone number listed for his address," she said. "You'll probably have to go there yourself."

Boggs looked over at the gurney again. "Yeah ... of course I will."

The nurse could read the disgust in Boggs' demeanor.

"Did you know this young man?" she asked.

Boggs hung his head and thought for a moment.

"I must have warned him... maybe warned is too soft... I must have *threatened him* a dozen times to stop street racing. But these kids..." Boggs motioned to Rager's corpse. "These kids have no respect for the law... or anyone for that matter."

Suddenly, the nurse was jolted -- her eyes becoming wild with alarm. Immediately, she hurried toward the gurney.

"This guy is alive! I saw a finger move!"

Boggs was stunned, suddenly finding himself wearing a deer-in-the-headlights look – the kind that only comes with clueless bewilderment.

As the emergency room became enveloped in a flurry of activity, Boggs could only lean against the cold brick wall and watch as doctors and nurses worked feverishly to revive Kent Rager.

With hat in hand, Boggs wobbled through the double glass doors and pulled a cigarette from his shirt pocket as he headed out to the emergency roundabout.

Woodward Avenue, Royal Oak – 1970

The early autumn twilight brought with it a golden sunset of bright orange clouds accented by rose-colored highlights. Numerous blackbirds – stragglers procrastinating against their extended trip to points south – perched in long rows atop power lines that ran north along the boulevard from Highland Park to the Pontiac Loop. Below the birds, colorful, dried maple leaves swirled along the sidewalks and curbs with each passing car.

A well-raked '69 Roadrunner swung into the left-hand lane on Woodward Avenue, its driver, Denny Stark, craned his neck in order to observe a tiny car idling next to him at the red light. It was a shining, baby blue Ford Pinto – the first model Denny had ever seen.

Denny noticed the Pinto's driver was actually a very pretty young lady with bright-colored beads in her long blond hair. Denny called them *hippie beads*.

Denny was well aware that hippie chicks didn't really go for gearheads, but he burped the throttle of his four-barrel Carter carb just enough to kick open the secondaries. The exhaust belched a menacing note that caught the girl's attention.

"Wow. Is that a 440?" she asked.

"Uh, no…." Denny hesitated. "It's a 383."

"Six-pack?" the hippie girl asked.

"Nope. Carter AFB, four-barrel" Denny replied, already spellbound by the girl's command of all-things-musclecar.

"Oh… well…" The girl trailed off. Apparently losing interest in Denny's performance options, she looked upward to the red traffic light and drummed her fingers on the wheel.

"It's got a cam," Denny offered.

"That's nice," she smiled without looking at Denny.

"What's your name?" Denny sputtered out just as the light went green.

"Green light. Gotta go," the girl grinned as she gunned her little Pinto across the intersection.

"Damn!" Denny yowled as he cuffed the steering wheel. "I *knew* I should have ordered the 440! What was I thinking?"

Despite the green traffic signal, Denny spent a few more seconds at the stop, contemplating his failure. He looked down at his hands, dismayed at what had just transpired. When Denny looked up again, a flash of bright purple caught his eye to his right; to be more specific: Plum Crazy Purple.

A brand new 1971 Dodge Challenger had rumbled to a stop where only moments ago a beautiful blond hippie girl had rejected Denny. Despite the green light, the purple Challenger rumbled ominously next to Denny's Roadrunner.

Denny looked over at the driver.

"He can't be more than 17 years old." Denny whispered as he observed the driver rolling down his window. The driver nodded to Denny before furtively looking about for any signs of police vehicles.

"Fifty?" the driver smirked.

Denny hesitated. "I'm not taking lunch money from a school boy."

"A hundred then?" the driver prodded.

"I don't have a hundred on me. Make it fifty," Denny huffed. "But you're gonna regret this, little boy."

As the light turned red again, both drivers sat. A long, uncomfortable silence ensued, until Denny broke the silence.

"So... what have you got under that purple hood, Junior?"

The young driver gave his Challenger a long rev before he turned a steely look to Denny.

"Pain."

"Oh yeah well... We'll see about that, won't we?" Denny chuckled.

Both drivers craned their necks to observe the traffic light facing east. They both caught a glimpse of yellow and began revving their machines with wild abandon – both trying to psyche-out the other one.

As the light went green, both cars roared off the line. Copious amounts of white smoke billowed from their rear wheel wells as hot rubber melted on frigid asphalt.

Sharing over 700 horsepower between them, the sound of their laboring engines was almost deafening as the two passed out of the intersection. They burst forward, slamming second gear almost simultaneously.

Pun intended; that's where the rubber met the road. The purple beast leaped forward, putting a car length on the Roadrunner in a split second.

"Oh, crap!" Denny yelled over the sound of his roaring piston-pounder.

As Denny slammed third gear, he witnessed the Challenger disappearing into a cloud of exhaust smoke, burned rubber and twilight's closing darkness.

Denny let up on the pedal and downshifted his 4-speed Hurst into third gear. He spied the Challenger at the next light. Unfortunately for Denny, the intersection was in front of Big Boy's Burgers. The Challenger pulled into the lot. Denny sheepishly maneuvered his Roadrunner into a parking spot and dug some cash from his jeans.

As Denny exited his car, he was stunned to see the same beautiful hippie chick walking out of Big Boy's with a large soda cup. It was only then that he noticed he was parked next to her baby blue Pinto.

"Nice one," the girl grinned as she took a sip from her drinking straw.

"You already know?" Denny puzzled.

"Word travels fast on the strip," she gave Denny a coy wink. "I'll give you an "E" for effort though."

"No thanks," Denny scowled as he marched away.

The purple Dodge was idling at the exit to Big Boy's lot. The young driver seemed to have no interest in accolades, exchanging war stories with other drivers or even a quick burger.

Denny gave a quick look around before passing his 50 bucks through the Challenger window.

"Man, I gotta hand it to you. That thing is quick with a capital K," Denny marveled. "What are you running under there?"

The young driver snatched the money from Denny's fingers.

"I told you already." The driver said as he stashed the cash into his shirt pocket.

"Pain."

TRAJECTORY

Kent Rager's body was launched through the open window of his speeding Mustang Boss 429 as it traveled at a speed of 100-plus miles per hour. As he exited the vehicle after the first roll, the Mustang had slowed to approximately 80 mph. At this point, Rager was flung skyward from the car window at a 30-degree angle. Perhaps still aware of his predicament at this point, Rager may have enjoyed a brief birds-eye view of the crash scene at 10 meters or about 30 feet above. Odds are better that Rager struck his head on the doorsill on his way out, so he would have looked more like a rag doll being launched from a catapult.

If Rager were conscious, his enjoyment might have been short-lived however, as the entire trip would have lasted but 2.04 seconds, covering 210 feet. This would put Rager's mangled body well away from the massive explosion of his Mustang's gas tank. But if Rager did smack his arrogant skull on the doorframe upon exit, he would have been measurably slowed down, thus his journey through the suburban skies of Detroit would have been much shorter.

Nonetheless, Rager had sustained no burns when examined at the scene by Sgt. Harlan Boggs a half hour after the incident occurred.

Because of Rager's penchant to wear black, nobody had actually witnessed his flight away from the rolling Boss 429 against a moonless night sky. All eyes were on the rolling mass of twisted black sheet metal and flying suspension  parts. Rager's impact upon the loose gravel of the construction area may have knocked him out cold, if he wasn't unconscious already, but it also would have knocked the wind out of him – perhaps even collapsing a lung.

And so it was that when Boggs discovered Rager's twisted body, he failed to detect any breathing. Boggs was not a trained medical technician, so he immediately draped a blanket over Rager's mangled corpse.

Out of professional respect, the arriving medical personnel took Boggs' word for it that Rager had died in the crash. (It was, after all, 1970.) They covered Kent in a sheet before rolling him on a metal gurney to the back of a Cadillac ambulance.

Meanwhile, back on the strip above, Tucker, Hoyt and Dawn spoke briefly with Boggs while waiting for a tow truck to haul away Tuck's '65 GTO. The rest of the crowd had scattered upon seeing Boggs' police cruiser and hearing the shots fired at Rager's speeding Mustang.

In essence, nobody at the scene that night had any idea that Rager had survived the crash. As far as they knew – and as word had it on the streets north of 8 Mile Road – Rager had been burned to death while trapped inside his Boss 429.

The only person who knew that Rager had survived the crash was Harlan Boggs, but there was no way Boggs was going to volunteer to the young baby boomer set on Woodward Avenue that he'd exercised poor judgment on the night of that infamous duel.

After ten days of unconsciousness, Rager awoke alone in the emergency ward at Montrose Memorial Hospital. He was later informed that nobody had come to visit him – not even his dear, old drunken dad. Rager reasoned that for his father to actually visit him in the hospital would have required leaving his couch, television and alcohol for a few hours.

Rager had broken an arm, both legs and ruptured his spleen in the crash. He had sustained a concussion, several lacerations to the head, neck and shoulders and had ruptured two vertebrae. It would be months before Rager would be released from Montrose Memorial Hospital and in the grand scheme of things in 1971, he'd already be just a bad memory to most street racers.

But Rager was far from finished with street racing.

CHAPTER 2

Montrose, Michigan 1971

The center of Montrose was typical of most northern boroughs in mid-March. Smog-blackened snow banks melted in the late winters warmth and would freeze again during the overnight chill. Municipal trucks would lay down more road salt and the cycle would be repeated. Lumbering cars would splash the dank salt water over the snow, while exhaust pipes belched-out carbon gobs of dark gloominess. Soon, the warming air would create a thick, dinghy fog that made the last few weeks of winter the most depressing of all.

"Spring is just around the corner," the locals would exclaim with much forced resolve, but those last weeks of winter were as tough to negotiate as the last few rounds of a prizefight. Sometimes just a hint of spring in the air was enough to break winters spell in the minds of hearty mid-westerners.

With hope springing eternal, the street sweepers would soon be out in force, bright purple crocuses would be poking through the remnants of the snow and the Detroit Tigers would be returning from sunny Florida. With any luck – and a great season from Mickey Lolich – Tiger Stadium might be hosting yet another World Series this year.

At Tucker Knox and Willie Hoyt's *Royal Oak Speed and Repair Service*, the signs of spring were already arriving. The aroma of grease, anti-freeze and 97-octane fuel created a hypnotic effect for any gearhead who happened into the garage area. Cars in all stages of completion crowded the garage, awaiting Hoyt's magical touch, which would transform them into the mean street machines that would menace Woodward Avenue and its surrounding byways in the coming summer months.

On warmer nights, some of the drivers were already braving the salted pavement and bringing out previews of their glimmering street machines. Cruising up and down the strip or parking these muscle cars in a line at Big Boy's Burgers offered yet another sign that winter was no longer welcome.

In the front office of the repair garage, Tucker Knox was rubbing his eyes as he labored over a spreadsheet. With no absence of frustration, he fired a pencil down at the paperwork and he rose from his desk. He opened the door to the noisy shop and beckoned to his partner, Willie Hoyt.

"Hey, Willie! Got a minute?"

The whining of an air gun abruptly stopped.

"Don't call me Willie, Tucker."

Tucker was in no mood. "Just get in here? Now?"

Sensing Tuck's frustration, Hoyt wiped his hands on a faded red shop rag as he entered the office.

"What's up, boss?" Hoyt knew Tucker loathed being called *boss*, but his feeble attempt at humor wilted under the heat of Tucker's concerned demeanor.

Tucker stood, hands on hips, staring out through the hazy glass window of his office. Hoyt was not just his best friend, he was like a brother to him– any confrontation between them was painful for Tucker to initiate. He took a deep breath and turned to his desk – not looking up at Hoyt.

"Hoyt, why are we charging out all of these gaskets? We have head gaskets, dome cover gaskets, oil pump gaskets, a *ton* of carb gaskets and gasket-gaskets. Why?"

Hoyt rolled his eyes and shook his head. "Tuck, we need those parts to keep the flow going out back."

Tucker looked down at the sheet and grabbed a stack of receipts.

"Hoyt, we can't afford to stock all these parts. Things are getting very tight around here. Besides, we don't have enough room out there."

Hoyt stepped forward and gazed down at all the receipts and charge slips.

"Tuck, if we have to run out and get these parts as-needed, or if we order them in from the parts store and wait for deliveries, we wind up wasting more time that could be better spent. I'd rather be fixing cars than chasing down parts around town."

Tucker nodded, but wasn't convinced. "Look, buddy, this UAW strike has the whole town upside down. The autoworkers aren't buying parts or fixing up their rides, because the money's become tight. Until they settle things with the Big Three honchos, we're all along for the ride on this rocky road to ruin."

Hoyt shook his head. "It's gotta end soon, Tuck. But trust me, it's cheaper to stock some of this stuff than it is to sit here waiting on it to arrive."

Soundly beaten, Tucker nodded in agreement. "Just tell me when you have to put in a large parts order, okay? I mean, we just need to keep an eye on everything. My dad ran this shop for 25 years without a hitch. We've been here for 8 months and we're already spilling red ink all over the spreadsheets."

"Whatever that means," Hoyt grinned as he opened the door to the cold garage. "Want to do a few oil and filter changes for me?"

Tucker looked up from his desk. "Yeah, man… anything to get out of this depressing office for a few hours. Let me grab my coveralls."
The two headed out into the cold garage.

* * * * * * * * *

Outside Montrose Memorial Hospital, a young nurse activated the handicapped door button and bumped an empty wheelchair over the threshold into the outpatient reception area.

At the reception desk, Betty Peterson watched a lone male figure outside the foyer. Oddly dressed in surgical scrub blues with a black leather jacket, the man dug out a pack of Lucky Strikes from an inside pocket and then lit a cigarette.

The young nurse approached Betty with a concerned look.

"Who *was* that guy?" the nurse asked.

Betty kept her eyes on the man outside. "I'm not sure, but I know he's been in here for months – almost died in a pretty bad car accident."

The nurse looked over her shoulder at the man outside. "He asked me out. It gave me the creeps. He's very handsome, but there's something evil in his eyes. When I told him I wasn't interested, he laughed and told me he'd be back."

Betty grinned nervously. "Really. That *is* creepy. Wait a second… let me look up his records."

Betty thumbed through her admittance files. "I know he arrived back in late summer. It was à Friday night, because I remember being really pissed-off about not being relieved by Brenda when my shift was over. She's always late. Anyway, a cop escorted this guy in. He was dead – or so they thought."

The young nurse listened intently to Betty, but furtively checked over her shoulder with the same trepidation a surfer would after spying a shark in the water.

Betty pulled a file out of a drawer. "Ah, here it is! Let me see here…."

The young nurse strained up onto her toes as she peered over the desk.

"Who is he?"

"His name is Rager," Betty answered. "Kent Rager."

"Rager," the nurse repeated. "My. How befitting."

* * * * * * * *

Standing beneath a raised Cobra Jet Torino, Tucker winced as hot, black motor oil ran down his fingers. He wrestled an oil filter from the underside of the 428 V-8 block.

"Oww! This oil is still hot, man!"

Hoyt chuckled as he tossed a shop cloth over to Tucker.

"It was outside all night. Battery was low. I had to run her for a half-hour to get her juiced-up again. Sorry, Tuck."

"Wait a second," Tucker grinned, "didn't I hear a *bunch of cars* running out there this morning?"

Hoyt was exposed. "Yeah, well..." He stammered. "I can't see bringing freezing cold engine blocks into this already cold garage to rob me of all my heat, because *Ebenezer Scrooge* – namely you – won't let me inch the thermostat over 50-degrees. So I use the hot engine blocks to help heat-up my shop."

Hoyt shrugged. "But I'm sorry about your fingers, man."

"It's okay," Tucker grinned, "I like it. Working out here takes me back to the good ol' days when we worked on cars for the sheer fun of it. You know, before I became *Ebenezer*?"

Tucker thought for a second as he lubricated the rubber O-ring on the new filter. "We always knew what was hot on the streets – who we had to beat. Remember?"

Hoyt looked up from under the hood of a Charger he was wrenching on.

"We still know, Tuck. We just never have time to talk about it anymore."

Tucker nodded as he screwed the filter into place. "So... tell me then. What's the latest from Woodward?"

Hoyt's face lit-up like a rear-ended Ford Pinto. He placed his wrench on the Charger's air cleaner and walked over to Tucker.

"Well, word on the street has it that there's one of those new Dodge Challenger R/T's done-up in that plum-crazy purple color. She's got a 440 in her with a six-pack, but word is the driver's just a lil' dork whose dad works for Chrysler – a big chief on the ol' Dodge totem pole, you know what I mean?

Tucker laughed. "So let me guess; the swinging-dick had the factory work-over the block and massage some extra ponies out of her."

Hoyt pointed at Tucker. "Exactly! *A lot* of *ponies* to be exact. The kid drives all the way in from Grosse Swank Shores, looking for some street action. He can handle any wager. I've heard he's even bet $500 on a running start quarter."

Tucker gave Hoyt a double take.

"Grosse Point? It figures. But come on, five hundred? That can't be true!"

Hoyt's eyes widened as he pushed his tale.

"No, man, I swear it's true. He put up the fiver, in cash too, but the other driver chickened out. That's why he's on Woodward. He used to run Gratiot, but the drivers chased him outa there. I heard they wanted to kick his ass."

"Wow," Tucker rolled his eyes. "I'd love to take-on that little chump with my Goat."

"No go, brother." Hoyt shook his head. "That R/T has some serious go-go juice underneath the hood. I wouldn't mess with that kid for any amount!"

Tucker stopped working - deep in thought for a moment.

"Well, who else has he beaten?"

"You won't believe this," Hoyt exclaimed with elation, "but the kid actually whipped Eddie Kendall's Chevelle SS 454 last Saturday night. It was a hundred-dollar flutter. Gone. Kendall was mortified."

"Wow. Anyone else?" Tucker asked.

Hoyt laughed. "Yeah, that 428 Cobra Jet Torino... you know, the one you're standing under right now?"

Tucker looked up at the underbelly of the Torino.

"The reason it's here is because Billy Lardner wanted me to work some magic on it. He lost eighty bucks to that same kid."

Tucker shook his head. "Then there's no hope?"

"There's one factor – a bad one." Hoyt explained. "The kid's crazy. Some say he can't drive, while others say he takes too many chances. He's got too much thunder underneath him and he's just plain dangerous."

Tucker walked over to the lift controls and cringed as deafening compressed air blasted out of the relief valve – lowering the Torino Fastback to the oil-stained cement floor.

"What about Boggs? Does he know?" Tucker shouted over the uproar.

"Oh yeah," Hoyt related. "Boggs is frustrated. Word has it the kid gets all of his speeding tickets fixed before they're ever filed. Daddy's got major connections in the city."

"Yeah and lots of Chrysler demos to hand out to willing police chiefs, I'll bet." Tucker offered.

No doubt," Hoyt huffed, "but Boggs thinks the old man knows the governor."

"That would do it." Tucker laughed.

Hoyt frowned. "Let's see the governor get the kid out of jail when he kills someone. I'm telling you, Tuck, this tool is bad news."

"I believe you, Hoyt." Tucker winked. "I'll try to stay away from purple Challengers."

"Heed the Hoyt!" Hoyt chuckled.

CHAPTER 3

Revival: Royal Oak, Michigan

Jerry Schultz worked feverishly on a mustard stain that mocked him from his new paisley tie. Dipping a napkin into a Dixie cup full of water, he frowned as sweat beaded from the brow of his oversized skull.

"Come on outa there, you son-of-a-bitch!" He cringed at the tie while his swivel chair creaked under the force of Jerry's three hundred-pound frame.

Jerry's frustrations may have seemed trivial, but they actually ran much deeper than just a mustard stain on a cheap, Val-U-Mart clip-on. His business, *Jerry's Honest Used Cars and Trucks* had been stagnant for almost 3 months. It had reached the point where he was no longer opening his mail. Jerry swore he could feel his blood pressure rising every time a tire-kicker walked off his lot without purchasing a car. Jerry's tiny, paneled veneer sales office was beginning to close in around him like a noose. With a wife and three kids at home to support, the endless days spent at his used car lot weren't even covering the expenses at his business – let alone his home mortgage.

In fact, business had become so abysmal that his wife, Nancy, had stopped asking him about his sales each night at dinner. Nancy figured that Jerry would arrive home for dinner with a smile on his face on the day he finally made another sale. In the meantime, Nancy was working a few days a week at the Sunrise Diner as a waitress for the breakfast and lunch shift; this kept food on the Schultz family's dinner table.

Jerry stood and quickly clipped on his wet paisley tie as he heard the sound of a burbling V-8 resonate across his car lot. Through the window he spied a weather-beaten, red '66 Chevelle SS slowing to a stop outside his door.

Three men exited the battered muscle car. Kent Rager leaned on a black cane as he eyed the collection of cars in Jerry's lot while his two moronic sidekicks, Stan and Ralph, sparked-up Lucky Strikes.

Jerry wasn't pleased with his latest sales prospects. "Now what?" he breathed.

Rager, neatly-trimmed in his black slacks and leather coat, stood in direct contrast to Stan and Ralph's filthy coveralls and long, scraggly hair.

Jerry drew a deep breath as he turned the doorknob to exit his office.

"What the heck do these clowns want?" he said aloud as he squeezed his rotundness through the narrow entry door.

Jerry put on his best smile as he waddled toward the threesome.

"Can I help you guys?" Jerry grinned nervously. "We've got some fantastic deals this week!"

Numerous encounters, all with identical endings, had worn Jerry's cheery façade quite thin.

Stan turned to the sound of Jerry's voice. "Yeah man, we're looking for something with major balls. You got anything like that here?"

Stan's head was immediately jerked backward by his ratty ponytail as Rager stepped forward. Stan stumbled back, falling against a '68 Plymouth Satellite.

"What did I tell you before we got here?" Rager hissed through clenched teeth.

Stan straightened his coveralls along with his miniscule dignity. "Yeah, I know, Rage. Sorry, man."

"Like the man said, we need something with some grunt. I'm talking about cubic inches and no more than two doors. You got that?" Rager stared coldly into Jerry's eyes.

Jerry had dealt with customers from all walks of life in his car sales career, but he'd never experienced the intensity of fear instilled by Kent Rager's fixed glare.

"Y-yes...yes I do," stammered Jerry. "I keep the good ones locked-up in the garage out back. Too many vandals and thieves, you know?"

Jerry made the mistake of glancing over at Stan and Ralph as he spoke the word "thieves." By the time he realized his error it was already too late.
Ralph flicked his Lucky Strike onto the hood of the nearby Plymouth. He grabbed Jerry's wet paisley tie and pulled Jerry's face up to his nose.

"What 'zactly you mean by *thieves*, porky?" Ralph's odiferous breath now complimented his raunchy appearance.

Jerry stood frozen, not knowing how to respond to Ralph's aggressive manner.
Rager cuffed Ralph's ear hard, causing Ralph to reel away in pain, which was well blended with a generous helping of drama.

"Ha, ha!" Stan laughed at Ralph's misfortune, but was quickly stifled as Rager glared at him.

Turning back to Jerry, Rager motioned toward the garage at the rear of the car lot.

"Sorry about the interruption..." Rager squinted at the nametag on Jerry's plaid sport jacket. "...Jerry. Let's see what you've got."

Despite being large, sloppy and disheveled, Jerry knew his cars and Rager was not there by accident. Word on the street was that Jerry Schultz had some *badass iron* hidden in his garage and Rager was curious to find just the right fit that would lead him back to dominance on Woodward Avenue and beyond.

Jerry unlocked the overhead garage door and grunted as he pulled the handle upward. Suddenly, the door was jerked upward quickly by Stan and Ralph who'd become as giddy as cherry wine-drunk schoolgirls at a sock hop. The door was tossed open under the combined lifting force of Jerry plus Rager's two anxious buffoons.

Inside the garage sat a dozen dust-covered samples of Detroit's  rapidly vanishing glory days. A 396 cubic-inch '68 Nova SS was perched at the front corner – a broken headlamp and dented front bumper seemed to be it's only failing.

Across from the Nova were two '69 Plymouths – a GTX and a Roadrunner Both had big blocks. But the Roadrunner was factory-tricked with a 426 Hemi and dual 4-barrel Carter carbs. This set up was worth 425 ponies on the street – right outa the box.

Further down the line, Rager spotted a blue 1970 Pontiac Trans-Am with a Ram Air IV 400 that caught his eye. Rager walked around the car twice, and then looked up at Jerry.

"How much for this monster?" he asked.

Jerry didn't have to hesitate. "This was a repo I grabbed on auction a few months ago, so it's ready to roll. It's only got 17-thou on the speedo, but it cost forty-four hundred new. I can let it go for thirty-four...firm."

Rager rubbed his jaw. "Thirty-four, huh?"

Rager walked the perimeter of the car once again.

"It's too... *blue*. What else you got?"

Jerry motioned to the back where a couple of faded Batman bed sheets obscured an unknown vehicle.

"Whoa. This looks interesting." Stan whispered as the foursome approached the car.

With a small degree of deliberation, Jerry grabbed the corner of the sheet and dramatically unveiled....

* * * * * * * * *

The young guns on Woodward Avenue claimed there was nothing mechanical that Will Hoyt couldn't make run faster and more efficiently. Nobody believed this more than Hoyt himself. But rather than displaying that confidence with a cocky attitude, Hoyt displayed a sense of humility and a down-to-earth demeanor.

Hoyt's God-given aptitude was offset by a general fear of all-things-female. Adding to that, Tucker often accused Hoyt of "not being able to joke his way out of a paper bag." Hoyt loved to laugh and tell long humorous stories, but no timing light ever created could fix his pathetic punch line technique.

Tucker often marveled at Hoyt's childlike demeanor. Hoyt shared his tales as if they were being heard for the very first time – delivered with wide-eyed enthusiasm and genuine laughter. There was nothing phony about William T. Hoyt and there wasn't an evil bone in his skinny little body.

And so it was that when people dropped their cars off at *Royal Oak Speed and Repair Service* they knew they were getting *the best of the best*. Tucker's father, Alvin Knox, had always been a straight shooter and his repair business thrived because of it. Tucker was a Vietnam veteran and a well-chiseled, athletic young man who held his father's values. These ethics, combined with Hoyt's mechanical wizardry, made the speed shop the only place to go in the minds of their loyal customers.

The *Gospel of Hoyt* was spreading throughout the land – or at least in the land just north of Detroit's 8 Mile Road. From Livonia to

Mount Clemens to Pontiac and down to Grosse Point Shores, anyone who wanted to improve their gas mileage, diagnose a problem or just go *really, really fast* would seek out Hoyt.

Despite all of this notoriety however, the repair shop was running in the red. The autoworker's strike of 1971 was creating financial hardship for many in the support trades and services, which fed the Big Three automakers. When the wheels ground to a halt on the assembly lines, the ripple effect reached across the entire Midwest. As long as a union strike was in progress, work was scarce for all.

Hoyt was a true wizard when it came to getting his work done quickly and done right. When simple fixes were required, Tucker would often roll up his sleeves and lend a hand, but more and more, Tucker found himself in the front office taking phone calls, writing work orders and chasing down elusive parts. In 1971, the microprocessor was introduced to the world, but it would be many years before it would arrive to help streamline Tucker's office workload.

Tucker kept a photo of his deceased brother, Chris, on his desk. He was now far enough removed from Vietnam to accept that the war had taken his only sibling from him. The pain he felt was slowly morphing into a numbness that Tucker felt was necessary in order for him to focus on life. When times got tough, Tucker would drop what he was doing and focus on Chris' photograph and ask himself, *what would Chris do?* More often than not, Tucker would find an answer by observing this simple ritual.

Other times, Tucker would simply pick-up the phone and dial Dawn's number. Dawn had a *no BS* attitude about most things, so when Tucker felt lost, Dawn would apply a simple redirect, which always set him back on track. But today was going to be different. By the end of this business day, Tucker, Hoyt and even Dawn would be angrily butting heads.

* * * * * * * *

By 1969, Ford Motor Company was neck-deep in the muscle car wars. With sales of the Chevrolet Camaro headed through the roof, Ford needed to equip its own pony car, the Mustang, with something extra special to compete with the Camaro SS 396.

The answer was the 429 block.

Offering a big block with a wide bore and hemispherical combustion chambers, the motor possessed an astonishing potential for raw horsepower. However, Ford's own performance guru, Larry Shinoda was disappointed with the finished product. Shinoda wanted a factory Mustang that would run 10-second quarter miles in factory trim, but the actual production Boss 429 just wasn't capable of such low ETs. Ford had mandated a rev limiter, a smaller carburetor than what was mounted on the Boss 302 and it was further choked by a restrictive intake manifold. When combined with a relatively mild solid lifter cam, and its restrictive exhaust system, all the potential horsepower of the 429 was bound and gagged. Basically, the 1969 Boss 429 was a monster chained and strangled by fear – a fear that it may have become *too powerful*.

So while the finished 429 was a ball-tearing beast, rated to 375 horsepower at 5200 RPM, the power band was narrow for an engine this big; all the result of the intake and exhaust restrictions.

However the secret was that Ford had intentionally underrated the Boss 429 for racing as well as to make the car insurance affordable for the consumer. Dyno testing showed the 429 to be closer to 500 horsepower – although at a very high rpm. It was rumored that yet another 100-125 horses were on tap once the four-barrel carburetor, intake, restrictive exhaust system and speed governor were removed or replaced.

Having street raced and worked his 1970 Boss 429 prior to his accident last summer; Kent Rager knew all of the idiosyncrasies of the engine. He knew where to find the extra juice that would vault the car from *mediocre* to *menacing*. So when Jerry Schultz pulled away his son's old Batman sheets to reveal a "Black Jade" 1969 Boss 429 Mustang, Rager thought he'd just died and gone to heaven.

The Mustang was immediately swarmed over by the thuggish threesome as Jerry stood back – still wishing in the back of his mind that these guys could actually come up with the cash to purchase his fine machine.

"Hey, Rage? It's got the "KK" sticker on the door!" Stan blurted excitedly as he slid behind the wheel.

Rager stood at the Mustang's nose and waited for Stan to stop fidgeting around inside the car. Once Stan realized Rager was glaring at him, he popped the hood release. Ralph was quick to step in and raise the hood. The two thugs inspected the engine.

"This thing is pure stock," Rager said before bumping his head on the raised hood when Stan tested the horn. Again, Rager glared at Stan.

"Oh,…sorry, Rage." Stan ears turned red with embarrassment – if not outright fear.

Ralph pulled his head out from under the hood and dressed his expression with his best intelligent façade. "It's got the Z-code on the block too, Rage."

Rager turned to Jerry, who was impatiently rocking on his heels. Apparently, the three hot dogs he'd scarfed down at lunch had quickly passed through his digestive tract.

"What's the damage on this beast?" Rager glared at Jerry, leaving little doubt that the price had better be more than fair.

Jerry rubbed his chin, already knowing what his price was, but the *selling game* had been initiated and Jerry was well practiced in his role.

"The sticker on this was pretty high – close to forty-six hundred," Jerry explained, "The Boss package was over twelve hundred alone."

Rager interrupted, "I know all-about the sticker pricing of these cars. Don't try to sell me on what the factory stuck on the glass. Just give me the damn price, Jerry."

Game over: Rager wasn't accepting the challenge. Jerry sighed, but fought back a smile. Rager was no tire kicker; he was a serious buyer.

"I bought this car from a very pissed-off father whose kid got one too many speeding tickets with it. He took the keys from the kid, drove in here and traded it in for cash and a Dodge Dart with a six-banger."

Rager fixed his stare on Jerry. He wasn't interested in small talk or any previous deals Jerry had been involved in. He wanted a price for the Mustang and was growing impatient.

Jerry sensed Rager's edginess.

"Look, I really need to get at least thirty-six firm for this one. The mileage is low, the car is bone stock and let's face it, with the new government emissions crap these hopped-up 'Stangs are already rare."

Rager reached into his coat and pulled out a wad of cash. Removing a few bills from the bundle, he tossed it over to Jerry.

"Here's thirty-two. Take it or leave it." Rager proposed.

Jerry's fat fingers gripped the wad of money, sending impulses through his nerve endings, which shot up through his flabby arms and into his gigantic head. It may not have been what Jerry wanted for the car, but God knows he only paid twenty-seven hundred for it. This cash would put food on the table, get the mortgage out of arrears, buy the kids new shoes, keep the business alive for another month and maybe even allow him to take Nancy to a movie.

But the salesman in Jerry wouldn't allow for a smooth transaction. "Another two bills and it's yours," he said with his best pasted-on smile.

Rager walked up to Jerry wearing a shit-eating grin. Jerry thought he just might have a deal, but Rager snatched the cash from Jerry's hand. He turned and motioned to his sidekicks.

"Let's go, boys. Mr. Clip-on doesn't want to cut a deal today."

Stan and Ralph sniggered like idiots as they passed by Jerry, but as they were about to exit the garage, Jerry changed his mind.

"Wait!" he cried. "It's a deal. I'll take the thirty-two."

Rager turned and walked back to Jerry, removed another bill from the roll and handed it to Jerry.

"Here's thirty-one hundred. I can play this game all day, Jerry" he said softly.

Jerry frowned. Money or no money, he wasn't about to get pushed around by some common street thugs.

"Wait a second! That's not fair, you offered...." Jerry wasn't allowed to finish his protest.

From the corner of his eye, Jerry saw Ralph's fist approaching his face at light speed, giving him no time to react. Pain rang through his jaw and into his head. Jerry's world spun around him as he staggered backward.

The force of Ralph's blow knocked Jerry back against a Buick Skylark GS while the immediate effect of lightheadedness dropped him to the floor. Jerry slammed upon the concrete like a large Ziploc bag full of Jell-O. The money flew in all directions into the air and fluttered down around his flailing body.

Judging by the rare display of a smile, Rager seemed to approve of Ralph's assault.

"So.... are we ready to draw up the paperwork, Jerry?"

Jerry nodded as he rubbed his jaw. Stan and Ralph grabbed him by his lapels and jerked him to his feet. They dusted Jerry's coat off with their hands.

"See that, Clip-on?" Stan offered. "We're pretty nice guys. I mean, once you get to know us."

The two morons giggled like schoolgirls as they helped Jerry toward the exit door. Minutes later, Rager bumped the stick into gear, burped the throttle and rolled another black Mustang Boss 429 out onto Woodward Avenue.

An old, yet all too familiar era had begun anew.

CHAPTER 4

Royal Oak, Michigan 1971

As soon as the sun dropped below the western horizon, the warmth of a March day in Detroit disappeared. The darker skies pushed out the warm and let in the cold. Old Man Winter was given respite for yet another evening.

Tucker shuffled papers and filed a few receipts in his office cabinet before donning his coat and heading out back to the garage.

At a greasy utility sink, hot steam emerged as Hoyt was making a futile attempt at scrubbing the black from under his fingernails with rough pumice soap.

"Hoyt, what do you say we grab a few burgers at Big Boys?" Tucker asked.

"What about Dawn?" Hoyt replied. "Isn't she coming with us?"

"She'll be here any minute," Tucker explained as he craned his neck to see out of the high shop windows.

"Are you guys waiting for me?" Dawn said as she rounded the corner from behind an old Ford Econoline van.

Dawn approached Tucker and gave him a peck on the cheek.

"How was your day, guys?" she asked.

Hoyt grinned as he wiped his hands with a shop towel. "It's getting a little bit better with each passing day," he grinned. "We'll be okay. Soon… I hope."

"Did I hear somebody mention Big Boys?" Dawn asked.

Just then, the steel entry door to the garage slammed shut. A young man approached the trio.

"Are you guys closed already?" he asked.

"Well, technically we're still open for five more minutes," Tucker said. "Can I help you with something?"

The young man grinned. "This is the shop where Will Hoyt works, right?"

"Yep, that would be me." Hoyt replied.

"Well, Mr. Hoyt, I've heard a lot of good things. I need some modifications done to my car and was wondering if you had time to fit it in?" he asked.

"Just speak to the boss man, Tucker," Hoyt winked. "He's standing right there with that pretty girl; the one who's way out of his league."

"You're *hilarious*, Willie," Dawn said sarcastically.

Tucker motioned to the young man. "Come into the office and we can set you up with a quote and maybe schedule some work," Tucker said.

Hoyt remained in the garage to remove his coveralls, while the three headed for Tucker's office.

"I tried the front door, but it was locked," said the young man. "I was hoping someone would still be here, so I tried the side garage door."

"Well, we're glad you did that," Dawn smiled. "By the way, I'm Dawn and this is the shop's proprietor, Tucker Knox. You already know our mechanic, Willie Hoyt."

"My name's Lucas. Lucas Fischer. You can call me Luke," he said. "I have a '71 Dodge I need to beef up a little."

"I'm sure we can help you go faster, Luke," Tucker offered. "What model is it?"

Luke walked to the office window. "It's right out here. The Challenger."

Tucker looked outside. His head jerked back slightly as he felt his blood run a bit colder.

"That car?" Tucker asked. "The purple one?"

"Yeah, that's the one," Luke smiled proudly. "Plum Crazy Purple."

* * * * * * *

Kent Rager maneuvered the Boss 429 down a narrow alleyway toward an old, dimly lit garage. In the alley, the exhaust note bellowed out with an additional echo effect, making it sound far more menacing.

As he pulled up to the old wooden garage doors they immediately swung open. Rager was fully expected.

A young black man with exaggerated Jimi Hendrix-style Afro hair directed Rager's Mustang into the garage and quickly closed the swinging doors behind it.

This was Quentin Seymour, Montrose Michigan's expert on all-things-Ford. If it sported the *Blue Oval*, Quentin could troubleshoot it, fix it, make it run better or massage it to run faster than ever. Like Hoyt, he lived and breathed high-octane fuel, but Quentin only knew Ford. He had no interest in Mopar, American Motors or General Anything.

Quentin's father had worked on Ford's assembly line from the early 1930s until he retired in 1965. Quentin got a job at Ford immediately upon graduating high school, but he wanted to work in R&D. Ford made a mistake in not allowing Quentin to help develop their engines. They required an engineering degree to be considered for that position, but Quentin ate, slept and breathed Ford engines and could dismantle and rebuild a 351 Cleveland while blindfolded. But without a degree, Quentin was relegated to the assembly line.

After hours, Quentin often cried in frustration when he thought of how Ford's mass produced engines could be improved upon, but he was never allowed to speak up. He filed suggestions over and over, but was stifled at every turn. Finally, after several years, Quentin quit Ford in frustration, but vowed to continue working on them and creating a better mousetrap – albeit a FoMoCo mousetrap.

Quentin had sent his resume to every NASCAR team that fielded a Ford in the late 60s, but he was never considered. Quentin knew it was mostly due to the fact that NASCAR was a "good ol' boy" network in the 60s, but he thought that perhaps he could be the *Jackie Robinson of stock car racing*. Unfortunately for Quentin, the race teams didn't see it that way.

Despite all of the blockades in Quentin's life, he found a niche for himself in his two-car garage just a few blocks away from Woodward Avenue. It was a popular hangout spot for the *Blue Oval Heads* during the warmer months but through the cold Michigan winters, Quentin labored alone by the warmth of a tiny, coal-burning stove. As it was with Hoyt, word spread like wildfire that Quentin was the best at what he specialized in and for Quentin Seymour, that specialty was *Forever Ford*.

Kent Rager always paid Quentin well for his work and for his willingness to go the extra mile without being asked. When Rager needed work done, Quentin immediately cancelled all other incoming projects so he could focus on Rager's machines. He didn't just get it right – he got it done as fast as any southern pit crew could ever hope to.

Rager popped the hood, exited the car and tossed a tightly wadded roll of cash to Quentin. "Parts and expenses," Rager explained. "If you need more, you know where to find me."

Quentin peeked under the hood for a few seconds.

"All stock. This baby's gotta breathe, man," Quentin exclaimed. "We need to open up the "in" and smooth the "out." Once we get that done we can think about other ways to make her run faster."

"You know what to do," Rager nodded. "How long?"

Quentin looked at the car while rubbing his chin. "Oh, I'd say by tomorrow night…late… *real late* though. I can pull the manifold and that crappy mini-carb out and drop the exhaust while I'm waiting on parts. Then it's just bolt and go, baby!"

"A cam?" Rager asked. "What about a cam?"

Quentin looked a bit perplexed. "C'mon, man! You don't wanna go pulling a solid lifter cam out 'til you see what we got with a its new lungs."

Rager was a bit taken aback. Quentin Seymour was the only person on earth to whom Rager allowed back talk. Stan and Ralph knew better than to question Rager about anything. But Quentin ruled over Rager with his knowledge – something Rager never questioned.

"Okay… sorry, Q," Rager said almost meekly. The last thing Rager needed was to lose Quentin. He knew that Quentin was his ticket to success on the streets and byroads around Woodward Avenue.

The ragged sound of Ralph's '66 Chevelle SS echoed down the alleyway.

"The ride's here. Gotta fly, man," Rager said as he exited a side door. "Good luck."

Quentin didn't hear Rager's goodbye – he was already deep under the Mustang's hood.

* * * * * * *

At Big Boy's Burgers, Tucker, Dawn and Hoyt waited patiently for their favorite waitress, Lenora, to take their order. Lenora had been at Big Boy's for a few decades and was like a second mother to many of the street racers and their squeezes that'd frequented the restaurant over the years. Some of the current patrons were actually the offspring of the early 50s street racers who frequented Big Boy's when Lenora was just learning the ropes as a waitress.

Lenora was now in her late-forties, but kept herself in good shape by constantly running from the kitchen to the restaurant booths over the course of her ten-hour shifts. In fact, with her bleached blond hair and short pink waitress uniform, many of the first-time male visitors often ogled her from behind; that was until she turned around to reveal her aging features. But Lenora was good-natured enough to realize when that mistake had been repeated and would often tease the younger guys.

"You boys see anything you like?" she'd ask as she handed them their menus with a coy smile and a wink.

Lenora always got it right. Every plate was served quickly and exactly the way it was ordered, so whenever Tucker, Dawn and Hoyt stopped by they'd always try to sit in Lenora's section.

Lenora approached the trio and immediately sensed some tension.

"You guys want the usual?" she asked as she began scribbling on her order pad.

Tucker looked down at his hands. Lenora stopped doodling and looked down at the threesome.

"Uh-oh. What's wrong, kids?" she asked with a look of deep concern.

"Oh, nothing we can't figure out," Dawn assured her with a forced smile. "Thank you, Lenora."

"Tell you what? I'll just get your usual order of burgers and fries. The way you like 'em," Lenora nodded. "And you kids work out whatever it is 'needs workin' out."

The hungry friends were facing a major dilemma that was causing some friction in their otherwise friendly circle.

Tucker was constantly looking at the bottom line of a speed shop that was running in the red for the first time since it opened its doors a few months after World War II ended. He needed every advantage and his trump card was Will Hoyt. With Hoyt's mechanical ability they could easily turn a wildcat like Lucas Fischer's purple Challenger into a hungry tiger. Tucker knew that Lucas had the money to pay for the work – and then some – which would nudge the shops needle off "empty" and give it some sorely needed running room.

Dawn, on the other hand, was adamantly opposed to this. She believed that nobody should so much as put a finger on the Challenger. To do so could scrve as a death sentence on the young Fischer boy.

Hoyt stood in the middle. He believed that Fischer was definitely a threat to himself and others, but also knew that he had to make things work in his partnership with Tucker. He wasn't about to refuse his lifelong friend and welcomed any challenge to make a car go even faster, but he also understood Dawn's concerns. The last thing Hoyt needed was to choose sides and drive a wedge between his friends.

All three were feeling the pressure of this decision. But it was Dawn who decided to step-up and address the issue.

"Look guys, let's settle this before the food arrives, please?" she begged. "We can still salvage a night of fun if we get past this."

"It looks like your mind is set, Dawn," Tucker offered. "If we decide to do the upgrades on Fischer's ride then we'll have you to answer to."

Hoyt allowed a nervous chuckle. "I'll say."

Dawn saw that as Hoyt's move toward Tucker. "Then you've already decided, Hoyt?"

"No… no, that's not true at all," Hoyt balked.

"Then which *is it* Willy?" Tucker probed.

Hoyt stared across the table at the couple, his face reddened under the weight of his decision.

"I'm not going to choose," Hoyt answered. "But Tucker's the boss and I'll do whatever comes out of that office on a work order."

"Fine then… it's settled," Dawn reacted with muted ire. "Looks like you'll be doing the work then."

"No, nothing's settled, Dawn," Tucker intervened. "We haven't reached that decision yet."

Dawn felt the tension lift enough to see an opening.

"Look, why don't we all sleep on it and just enjoy our dinner together?" She offered.

"Sounds good to me," Hoyt shrugged.

Like the *Lone Ranger*, Lenora arrived just in the nick of time with a large tray of plates and tall glasses of cola – all surrounding a large mound of golden French fries.

"This oughta sooth what's ailin' you kids!" she said with a cheerful tone. "It's okay to smile again!"

Lenora doled out the plates of burgers and slid the large mound of fries to the center of the table.

"Now brighten up and eat!" she ordered.

With grins all around, the three friends dug into their dinner.

* * * * * *

The mounds of snow banks had almost magically dissipated over the past few warmer days and, save for a few scattered pools of salty black water, the strip was relatively clean and inviting to even the most discerning motorhead. In 1970, road salt could eat-up a car in a matter of just a few years if the owner wasn't diligent about controlling the salt residue on its body and undercarriage.

The night seemed abuzz with flashing, roaring American muscle cars of all makes and models. Standing outside of Big Boy's Burgers, Hoyt closed his eyes and drank-in the symphony of distant thunder. The echo of far away cars revving and roaring on the boulevard put a smile on his face.

Hoyt reached forward and tugged on Tucker and Dawn's elbows.

"Stop!" he said, "and listen to the sounds of Woodward Avenue. It's absolutely beautiful." He closed his eyes again – still holding onto his friends' arms. Smiling widely, he shook his head. "Now *that's* what I call beautiful music! It's a concerto of raw American horsepower beating down on cold pavement. Ground pounders! I mean, you can almost *smell* the rubber burning off countless sets of spinning tires all over northern Detroit."

Dawn gave Hoyt a cross-eyed glance. "You know, Hoyt? You really are kind of kooky."

"More like eccentric," Tucker chuckled.

"Get in touch with your inner gaskets, man." Hoyt clucked in his best hippie speak. "Man, you gotta feel the groovy vibe of the wild horses!"

And as Hoyt spun around in his best Woodstock hippie dance, a brand new Orbit Orange 1970 GTO Judge rumbled loudly to the stoplight in front of Big Boy's.

"Holy cow!" Hoyt yelled in shrill exhilaration. "That's *exactly* what I'm talking about! That could well be a Ram Air *Four* Judge!"

Dawn and Tucker looked to the strip in dazed amazement. The Judge glistened in the reflection of the huge neon "Big Boy's Burger" sign.

"Wow!" They both blurted simultaneously.

As the light turned green, the Judge lumbered forward, with paint and chrome gleaming and a finely tuned exhaust note that drowned out every other sound on the street.

"Amazing." Tucker whispered as the Judge moved out.

* * * * * *

What Tucker, Dawn and Hoyt couldn't see was what happened just three sets of lights away.

The Judge rolled up to another stoplight in front of a closed pharmacy. The Judge's driver, Tommy Clark, had only purchased the '70 GTO just three days before. From the Royal Oak Pontiac dealership, he'd driven directly to Milt Schornack's new shop for some Bobcat upgrades.

From the darkness of the unlit lot, two headlights blinked on, followed by the unmistakable, split-second gear whir and familiar rumble of a starting Mopar V-8.

Within seconds the shadowed Chrysler cackled through the lot and onto Woodward Avenue. It blurted a sudden burst of RPMs, which lunged it forward, along side the Judge.

Tommy looked to his right and saw the car: a bright purple Challenger RT, 440, six-pack. The driver rolled his window down; a steely look was pasted on his young face. It was Lucas Fischer.

"Light-to-light for fifty clams?" Luke asked.

Tommy hedged, but looking at Luke's smug grin rubbed him against the grain.

"Gimme a break, man," Tommy nodded. "I just bought this Goat. I'm still broke."

Lucas chuckled, "Okay, how about twenty-five?"

Tommy sighed and contemplated his finances.

"Unless you're chicken shit," Luke laughed with maddening arrogance.

This really grated Tommy. Like Tucker, Tommy had only been home from his tour in Vietnam for a few months.

"Make it fifty, dipshit," Tommy blurted.

With that throwdown, windows were rolled up and both cars began their ritual of starting line intimidation. Motors were amped-up to 3,000 RPM. Both drivers stood on their brakes to hold the line, but no drum brake could stop the energy transfer as driveshaft torque began hopping their rear tires.

Tommy craned his neck to catch a glimpse of reflected yellow warning light from the cross traffic signal. Upon seeing the yellow, Tommy looked over the hood for the green – not even chancing the split second he might lose should he look over at the Challenger.

As the light turned green, an explosion of sound filled the night. High revving engines on wide dual pipes blasted out their murderous note, while spinning tires screamed in agony as they burned wildly from the friction against cold pavement.

Tommy jumped ahead with the advantage of Pontiac's notorious low-end torque, but by the time he banged second gear, he could see the purple Challenger's nose jumping in his passenger side window. Tommy anticipated his third-gear shift, but let the big Ram Air engine wind up a little higher to almost red line before he jammed the stick forward into third. Suddenly, the cars were even but the Challenger was gradually inching forward as both cars screamed along the boulevard at a scorching hot clip.

Tommy looked down at his shift knob and was both flabbergasted and elated simultaneously; he'd left the VOE knob closed! With the vacuum operated exhaust control open, the baffles inside the two exhaust mufflers would be angled back, not only to relieve some back pressure, but it also made the GTO sound even more menacing than it was already.

"Ah-haaaa!" Tommy cried out with joy as he yanked the knob outward.

The relatively small amount of horsepower Tommy gained was just enough to move him even with Lucas' Challenger again. As both drivers slammed fourth gear however, Tommy's Judge darted ahead of the Mopar by a bumper length.

Lucas was far from happy about losing his lead over the Judge. With the next intersection rapidly approaching, he knew he was about to lose the race. With all immaturity and bad intent, Lucas swung directly behind the GTO in order to attempt a draft that just might propel him back in front, but with the end looming only a few hundred yards away, he swung out too soon – clipping the right side corner of the GTO's bumper.

Tommy felt the nudge, then felt his rear end cutting loose. He swung the wheel frantically in a feeble attempt to steer into the slide as he was forced to jam his brakes on. The Judge swung its tiger tail too far left as it jackknifed and crossed into the opposing lane.

The left rear tire jumped the street curbing. Tommy felt the sudden jolt and heard a sickening crunch as his rear quarter sideswiped a speed limit signpost.

Tommy regained control and crossed back over the strip again. Banging on his steering wheel, he watched as the Challenger blasted through a yellow light at the intersection. It was quite apparent that Lucas and his Challenger were high-tailing it out of town. Tommy stopped for the red light and jumped out to assess the damage.

The rear quarter panel was dented and scraped from the rear seat window back to the bumper. Tommy looked back up the road toward the Challenger, which was now little more than a purple dot, far down Woodward Avenue.

"I'll catch up with you again, you little son-of-a-bitch!" Tommy screamed as he shook his fist.

Tommy climbed back into his Judge and u-turned back toward town; his car and ego equally damaged.

CHAPTER 5

10PM – Somewhere off Gratiot Avenue, Michigan 1971

Quentin Seymour silently rolled the Boss 429 Mustang down the slight decline of a dark alleyway and turned left onto Gratiot Avenue heading northeast. As the beast's momentum began to decrease, Seymour activated the headlights, turned on the ignition and popped the clutch. The Mustang burped, stalled, and then came alive as it ignited eight cylinders, which awakened like a bellowing giant from a terrifying dream. Quentin gave the pedal a few punches to clean out the chambers as black, oily exhaust snorted from the rear pipes. In short order, the pipes blew clear exhaust and Quentin applied more throttle. The Boss 429 had been brought back to life and – judging by the sound of its exhaust note – already ruled over all-things-automotive on Gratiot Avenue.

The rebirth was complete.

Quentin punched the gas and cruised along Gratiot like an F-15 fighter looking for a kill zone target. But the Q knew better than attempting to challenge another car; this was Rager's ride and if word got back that Quentin was racing in the Boss, Rager's response would not exactly be mild.

Instead, Quentin took the long route and headed north, then west on Highway 696, where he was able to really open up the Mustang and wring it out. From there, he'd hopefully meet up with Rager at Big Boy's, get paid, and catch a ride back from Stan. But Rager wasn't at Big Boy's – at least not yet.

* * * * * *

The outside décor of *The Rotary* nightclub left something to be desired – unless one had an affinity for T-111 siding, overflowing garbage cans and faded redwood stain. A well out-of-kilter shack had been built around the front entry in order to keep patrons from being snowed-in. It's sickly mismatched powder blue color had been applied after a loose can of paint was found in a back storage room. From outside, the pounding resonation of a tone-deaf rock band could be heard through the plywood walls. The bar was celebrating its one-millionth rendition of "Mustang Sally."

The lot itself was pitted with numerous black water potholes and was littered with chunks of loose pavement. Years of harsh winters with no spring maintenance efforts had left the lot looking like a lunar surface. A lone 100-watt floodlight illuminated the front of the single story, flat-roofed dive.

In the corner of the lot, Stan puffed on a Lucky Strike as Rager stared intently at the cars in the parking lot from the passenger seat of Stan's tattered '66 Chevelle SS.

Ralph exited the rear seat and stood outside the car.

"When we hear the music stop, it's show time," Rager stated calmly. "You know what to do."

"Gotcha, boss," Ralph said with some degree of trepidation.

48

Ralph hiked up his trousers a bit and headed inside the raunchy nightclub.

Rager gazed across the lot. "Okay Stan, pull around back next to that yellow Z-28. That's our baby."

Stan fired-up the Chevelle and slowly nudged the car behind the building.

Inside the bar, Ralph slapped a dollar bill down on the bar and nodded to the bartender.

"Pabst," he said as his eyes darted nervously around the bar.

On the tiny, crowded dance floor, Ralph spotted a redheaded *hippiette* wearing a headband, love beads and a tie-dyed tank top. He pulled a swig off his bottle of beer as he sized her up along with her dance partner. Her male counterpart's long curly locks, John Lennon glasses and oversize peace sign necklace screamed "Woodstock."

Ralph grinned and took another swig of beer as he leered at the redhead. He wiped his mouth with a grimy sleeve before venturing out onto the dance floor.

Ralph approached the redheaded hippie. "Hey baby! What do you say I cut in with you?" Ralph chortled through yellow teeth.

"Go away, dude," the male hippie ordered. "The chick's with me, man."

"Oh c'mon, dude!" Ralph protested. "Share the love, baby! It's all groovy, you know?"

"No," the hippie guy answered. "She's only dancing with me, brother. Back off."

Ralph nodded for a second as if he'd accepted the hippie's warning.

"I ain't your brother, you smelly hippie!"

Ralph swung hard and round-housed the hippie to the jaw. The hippie dropped and was out before he hit the floor. Ralph turned and grabbed the redhead by her wrists.

"Let's dance, baby!" He laughed as spittle of drool ran from one corner of his mouth.

"Leave me alone!" she cried as she struggled with Ralph's grimy grip.

The music abruptly stopped as the band looked on at the ruckus. As Ralph attempted to wrestle with the redhead, a man jumped on Ralph's back.

Outside, Rager heard the music stop; the planned distraction was underway and nobody would be exiting the honky-tonk for the next few minutes.

"That's our cue." Rager said calmly. "Ralph's in the shit. Let's get busy."

Stan approached the Z-28 and screwed a slide hammer into the door lock. He jerked the hammer weight back and easily popped the lock off the door panel. Inserting a screwdriver, Stan had the car door open in less than twenty seconds.

As he pulled the door open, Rager slid into the driver seat. Stan handed the slide hammer to Rager, who quickly screwed it into the ignition key slot and jerked away the mechanism. He turned the wheel from side to side.

"Okay, it's unlocked! Gimme the screwdriver!" Rager ordered.

Stan grabbed the slide hammer out of Rager's hand and slapped the large flathead into it. Rager pushed the screwdriver into the opened steering column and turned it. The car's V-8 fired immediately.

"Don't forget Ralph!" Rager barked as he closed the door and gunned the car out of the lot.

Rager put the pedal to the floor and burned an "S-curve" down the dark highway – with headlights still off – until he was far enough away from the bar.

Stan pulled the Chevelle around to the front of *The Rotary* and leaned over to shove open the passenger door. Like clockwork, Ralph scurried from the bar. Ralph's face was bloodied and a half-dozen angry bar patrons were in close pursuit. A beer bottle whizzed by Ralph's head and smashed against the roof sill of Stan's Chevy.

Ralph dove into the front seat just as Stan slammed hard on the gas pedal; spraying loose chunks of gravel and asphalt all over Ralph's pursuers.

Ralph rolled down the window as they bolted down the highway. He leaned out and waved.

"Eat shit, you dirty hippies!" Ralph screamed with a raucous laugh.

The bar patrons stopped and headed back inside. It was just another night at the local watering hole for them.

* * * * * * * *

The winter had not been kind to the rusted corrugated steel garage that was set back behind an aged storage warehouse. Rust had worked its way up to eye-level where plows had pushed giant mounds of salty snow against the siding as they cleared the parking lot.

Rager pulled the stolen Z-28 up to the garage door and beeped his horn twice, then once more a few seconds later. The door was raised quickly. Rager drove into the garage fast and the door was closed as quickly as it was opened.

Inside, Dick Sturgis was munching on a thick ham sandwich as he approached the Camaro through his busy chop shop. Rager climbed out and ran his hand along the edge of the front fender.

"This one's a beauty," Rager gushed with his best, pasted-on grin. "You'll sell these parts in a single day."

Sturgis nodded at Rager as he walked slowly around the Z.

"You know, Kent? For once you might be right," Sturgis grinned as he assessed the cars worth.

"The 302 cubes alone should fetch you a G-note, Sturg," Rager offered. "And the seats, body panels and chrome are like brand new – all around."

Sturgis nodded again. "I don't think this car's seen a day of winter. It's definitely a garage queen."

"So what are we talkin' here?" Rager asked.

"I'll give you two for it," Sturgis said without looking at Rager.

"Screw you, Dickie!" Rager blurted. "This thing is mint! And you said you wanted a '69 Z with a 302. Shit man, you even said you preferred yellow."

Sturgis ripped another large mouthful of ham sandwich from his mitt as he sized-up the car further. Then he spit a chunk of ham onto the floor.

"I hate fat." he shrugged. "Disgusting."

Rager boiled; knowing Sturgis was waiting him out.

"C'mon, make me a reasonable offer. I've got things to do"

Sturgis scarfed down his mouthful of ham and cheese and looked at Rager.

"Okay, twenty-two's my final offer... and it's only because that's all I have in the ol' cash box right now," Sturgis said.

"Twenty-seven," Rager replied. "Let's get this done, I've gotta split, man. My ride's here."

Just as Rager uttered his last sentence, the unmistakable untuned cackle of Stan's '66 Chevelle shitbox could be heard outside.

"I told you, twenty-two is all I have here, Kent." Sturgis pleaded. "Take it or leave it."

"Fine." Rager bit his lip.

Sturgis dug out a wad of bills, which Rager snatched from Sturgis' hand as he headed for the door.

Sturgis called after him, "You need a receipt with that?"

Rager couldn't help but laugh. "Now *that* was funny, Dickie!"

Rager exited through the side entry door as Sturgis turned toward his shop workers. "I want this thing torn down by 3AM," he yelled over the din of hissing air guns and a distorted AM radio, which was doing it's best to amplify "Spill the Wine" by *Eric Burdon and War*. "This Camaro is hotter 'n hell, so I want it to evaporate. Got it? And turn that damn radio down, you friggin' clowns!"

* * * * * *

It was just after midnight when Doug Rhoades stumbled out of *The Rotary Pub* with the newly found love of his life, Priscilla. Doug had asked Priscilla for a dance after a few courage-inducing brews and they'd danced and drank the evening away. Doug was encouraged by the fact that Priscilla was more of a gearhead – as opposed to the more common *peacenik chick* of the day. As a hard-working construction carpenter, Doug was tired of the *peace and love* baloney. His desire for Priscilla had intensified as the night wore on.

Doug offered Priscilla a ride home and had plans to bring her to the one room cottage he rented and ply her with a few shots of Mohawk Blackberry Brandy before seducing her. Coincidentally, Priscilla was secretly hoping that Doug was harboring that same intent.

The couple exited the bar and rounded the corner into the unlighted side of the rundown dive. Doug decided he needed an indication of how the evening would progress. He pushed Priscilla against the building and planted a short kiss on her lips. When Priscilla smiled and placed her arms around Doug's neck, Doug went in for the extended version. As they kissed, Doug pushed his body against her and was pleasantly surprised when Priscilla began slowly gyrating her tight blue jeans against his. Doug began wondering if he even needed any blackberry brandy now.

As others began exiting the rear parking lot, headlights illuminated the early spring love scene. Drivers began reacting with good-natured horn blasts and catcalls, which pressed Priscilla – still kissing Doug – to respond with a raised middle digit. As the last car rolled away, someone yelled the obligatory standard, "Hey, you two should get a room!" Doug decided there were warmer places to be enjoying their tryst.

"Let's get outa here," Doug grinned as he pulled Priscilla's hand and turned toward….

Nothing.

"What the hell?" Doug screeched, his voice breaking girlishly high from the shock. "My Camaro is gone!"

Priscilla moved up next to Doug, now a little more drunk than he was. A stolen car can be a real buzz kill.

"Wait a second," she puzzled, "do you *really* have a new Z-28."

But Doug was too upset to hear Priscilla.

* * * * * *

Tucker maneuvered his dad's aging Ford F-100 pickup truck into the speed shop's parking area. The old truck ran like a top, but was a little too well ventilated from rusted holes and misaligned doors and windows. Tucker blew on his hands to keep them warm. The heater worked, but couldn't keep up with the cold morning air. As he exited the truck, he eyed Luke Fischer's purple '71 Challenger parked in front of the garage entry door.

"What the hell is this?" Tucker uttered as he headed for the garage.

Inside, Hoyt had his hands wrapped around a large Styrofoam cup of hot coffee. "It's cold in here this morning, ain't it?" Hoyt offered – fully recognizing the distress on Tucker's face.

"What is that Challenger doing here?" Tucker demanded.

"Hey, don't look at me." Hoyt shook his head. "It was dropped off early. There were keys and an envelope shoved through the mail slot. I put them on your desk."

Tucker entered his office to find the keys and envelope. He tore the note open and found a short stack of fifty-dollar bills and a penciled note.

> *Dear Mr. Knox,*
> *I had to drop the car before school. I have enclosed $500 for the parts and labor to fix my car. Just let Mr. Hoyt do his thing. Let me know if you need more. I will stop by after school. Please do not call my house about this matter.*
> *Thank you,*
> *Lucas Fischer*

Tucker spread the cash across his desk. Part of him was elated at receiving a down payment that would really help edge the shop ledger back in the black, while his heart was wrenching over Dawn's objection to turning the kid's car into a virtual death trap.

Tucker turned toward the photograph of his brother.

"What would you do, Chris?" he asked.

Hoyt walked in at that exact moment. "Should I pull that Mopar in or not?"

Tucker took a deep breath then exhaled a sigh. "Yeah, we may as well. I don't see how we pay our bills if we turn it away."

"Hey, I'll knock it out fast," Hoyt winked. "Who's to know but us and the kid, right?"

Tucker looked down and nodded. "Yeah…" he sighed. "Who's to know?"

* * * * * *

The sun was setting over the strip as Denny Stark rolled his '69 Roadrunner into Big Boy's lot. As most drivers would, Denny disengaged the transmission and popped a few blurts of horsepower through the exhaust as he maneuvered in his spot. This was the unspoken "Hello, I've arrived!" rule of the late 60s and early 70s. Denny had decided to forgo changing out of his work clothes and go directly to the Woodward Avenue burger hangout from work. It wasn't so much of a conscious decision as it was the grumblings of a twenty-four year old male's empty stomach. Denny always summed up his needs in order of importance.

"Food, cars, girls – food, cars, girls!" he'd chant to his friends. "That's all we're about at our age."

Denny had no idea that this evening would cover all three of his basic needs. As he cut the ignition to his rumbling '69 Roadrunner in the parking spot, Denny spotted the blonde hippie girl's new baby blue Ford Pinto.

Doing did his best to straighten his hair in the rear view mirror; Denny exited his car and made a beeline for the restaurant. His head was filled with spinning cheeseburgers, fries and the possibility of meeting up with his dream girl again.

As Denny entered the busy diner, his eyes scanned the buzzing crowd. People were gathered in groups according to what make or model car they preferred. In one corner, the Z-28 boys were gathered – all sporting matching coats with the Chevy Bowtie on their backs. There were a few booths where only followers of the Blue Oval would dare venture and another smaller group of American Motors fans traded stories of their AMX engines. Each group was alive with the drone of voices relaying their tales of battle. It was war out there, a horsepower war and the never-ending battles raged on from street to street, night after night.

A soundtrack backed all of this noise from a jukebox at the far end of the diner, which was churning out "Joy to the World" by *Three Dog Night*.

Denny spotted the blond girl, who was sitting alone in a booth as Lenora took her order. He slowly worked his way through the mix of gearheads and groupies, but as he approached her table, he took a moment to gather her into his memory.

With some trepidation, Denny took a deep breath, checked himself over and stepped up to the blond hippie girl's booth.

"Hi! Remember me?" Denny smiled – hoping for her eyes to light up just a tiny bit.

The blond girl looked him over. "Nope, I can't say I do" she replied.

Denny's could feel his heart thump against the soles of his shoes as it dropped. But suddenly, a spark of recognition blazed in the blond girl's eyes.

"Oh wait, you're that dude with the 383, right?"

Denny was elated. "Yes! The Roadrunner! So you remember?"

The blond girl tried to hide her laughter at Denny's excitement.

"Would you like to sit down?" she smirked. "I love how you went all-out on tonight's wardrobe choice!"

Denny didn't respond. He slid next to her, his smile as wide as Anchor Bay.

"So, what's your name anyway?" Denny asked.

"Alison," she replied. "Do you have a name? Or should I call you *383*?"

Dennis giggled nervously. "I'm Dennis, but my friends call me Denny." Denny was trying – and failing – to hide his exuberance.

Suddenly, Lenora appeared again. "Are you going to sit there grinning like a love-struck school boy?" Lenora blurted over the noisy diner. "Or are you going to order something?"

"Oh, yeah… definitely," Denny could feel his face flushing red. "I'll just get the usual. Extra ketchup, please."

Alison stared at Denny for a moment. "You're kind of a strange dude, aren't you?" She shook her head as she watched his reaction.

Denny could see where the conversation was going yet steamed ahead anyway. "Look," he said frankly. "I am a little nervous around you. I'll get over it in a few minutes. Just bear with me, okay?"

Alison smiled. "Yeah man, that's groovy. I'll let you feel your joy. Besides, it's kind of cute – in a strange kind of way."

Denny wasn't certain what Alison meant.

"Thanks… I think."

CHAPTER 6

Darkness Falls

Tucker folded an envelope containing the day's receipts and placed it into an inside pocket of his coat. He walked through the doors to the garage and gave a shout to Hoyt, who was sweeping up piles of speed-dry in the darkened garage.

"Hoyt! I'm heading to the bank before it closes. We've got to get this cash into our account in time to pay the bills."

"I'll meet-up with you at Big Boy's in a half hour then?" Hoyt shouted back in his typically cheery demeanor.

"See you there, buddy!" Tucker called out.

As Tucker disappeared into the office again, Hoyt heard the garage door slam behind at the far end of the shop. It was Lucas Fischer.

"Hello, Mr. Hoyt!" Luke yelled. "Is the Challenger ready?"

"You're lucky. We were about to close up shop." Hoyt motioned to a greasy wooden square on the wall. "The keys are on the board. Car's in the back."

"So she's ready to go?" Luke asked.

"All set," Hoyt replied. "You be the judge. Let me know if you're not happy with the extra ponies you've got under that hood."

Luke smiled. "I'll be back for more!"

Luke snatched the keys from the board and headed back outside with another loud slam of the spring-hinged metal shop door. Hoyt grinned to himself as he envisioned Luke's initial reaction to the sound and performance of the Challenger's 440 engine.

Hoyt continued sweeping but heard the door slam again.

"Sorry, we're closed," he yelled to the far end of the shop. But as Hoyt turned, he saw Dawn; her arms folded, an angry fire blazed in her eyes.

"You guys did it, didn't you?" Dawn steamed.

"Did what, Dawn?" Hoyt asked.

Hoyt attempted to be coy, but Dawn wasn't buying it.

"You juiced-up that kid's Challenger. I just saw him climbing into the car out back."

"Look, Dawn... I..." Hoyt was flabbergasted.

"This is not cool! If that boy dies or kills somebody, you and Tucker are going to have blood on your hands!" Dawn was on fire. "Can't you see you've handed him a loaded gun?"

Hoyt stood frozen; his head hung down in a mix of embarrassment and fear of saying the wrong thing. Hoyt was known for having bouts with bad timing and he was determined not to let this time be one of them.

"Is Tucker in the office?" Dawn demanded.

"Well," Tucker said sheepishly, "don't you think he'd be out here by now once he heard the yelling?"

"Don't be a smart ass, Hoyt!" Dawn roared. "We talked about this and I'm very pissed-off that you guys went ahead and ignored my concerns."

Hoyt breathed out a deep sigh. "He went to the bank to get a deposit in. Look, if it helps, he had nothing to do with it, he…"

"Don't lie for him," Dawn bellowed. "He knew what was happening here and he could have stopped it."

"We needed the money, Dawn." Hoyt offered. "We were in a bind."

Dawn thought for a moment. "Blood money," she said before she turned and stormed for the door.

"Are you meeting us for dinner?" Hoyt called after her.

"Hardly!," Dawn sneered as she marched away – slamming the door behind her.

* * * * * * *

Denny beamed as he eyed two of his most favorite things; Alison, the gorgeous, newfound object of his desire and the half-pound of greasy, cheese-smothered burger that sat between a saucer-sized bun in front of him. He decided that life had not offered too many better moments than this.

Alison nonchalantly nibbled on a french fry as Denny peeked at her from the corner of his eye, but all that was about to change.

"Hey, Knob." A loud, startling voice called out to Denny, breaking his temporary Nirvana.

Denny looked up to see Kent Rager looming over him. Rager tapped the knurl of a walking cane on the table. "Is that your baby-shit orange Roadrunner out there in the lot?" Rager demanded.

"Y… yeah," Denny stammered, having immediately recognized Rager's chiseled features. "Why?"

61

"Well, scrote," Rager whispered. "I don't think you set your brake." Rager shook his head with false concern. "You know... you could *really* hurt somebody."

Denny stood up quickly to challenge Rager, but his attention was quickly drawn to the window. To Denny's dismay, the parking lot was mired in confusion as people scrambled to avoid his backward rolling, driverless Plymouth.

"What the hell?" Denny cried as he scurried from the table. "That's my ride!"

As Denny sprinted for the door, Rager turned his attention to Alison. Pushing Denny's food aside, he sat down next to her and extended a hand.

"Poor guy," Rager feigned concern, "such a loser."

Rager directed a steely look into Alison's eyes. "Kent Rager," he offered. "The pleasure's all mine."

Outside the diner, Denny sprinted past Hoyt's arriving Duster 340 as he attempted to catch his Roadrunner before it rolled out onto Woodward Avenue. Over the horrified screams of the people watching the scene unfold, the raucous guffaws of Stan and Ralph could be heard. The two buffoons were doubled over with laughter as they leaned against Alison's Pinto, leaving greasy smears on the light blue paint with their filthy coveralls.

Amongst the confusion, a bellowing Duster 340 cruised by the mayhem. Hoyt craned his neck as he watched Denny dive through the window of his Plymouth.

"What the heck is going on here?" he wondered aloud as he maneuvered into a parking space.

Denny was able to jam the brakes on within a few feet from the traffic flowing along the strip behind him.

"Son of a bitch!" Denny screamed as he dug through his pockets to find the keys to his Roadrunner.

Finding the ignition key, he jammed it into the dashboard and the 383 mill burped into service. Denny pressed down on the gas pedal and catapulted the car away from the dangerous road behind him. Maneuvering the Plymouth back into its original spot, Denny rolled up the windows and double-checked the parking brake before he locked the doors and exited the car.

Denny hurried back toward the diner, hoping his burger – and Alison – hadn't grown cold. But as he approached the entry to Big Boy's he spotted Alison through the plate glass window; she was nodding intently as Kent Rager talked with her. Denny's heart sank again as Alison caught his eye. Through the window, she smirked, shrugged and shook her head, as if to say, "Oh well," then turned back to her conversation with Rager.

Denny turned away and sulked back to his Roadrunner. There was one of those new *McDonald's* hamburger stands a mile down Woodward Avenue and Denny decided tonight might be a good time to sample their offerings.

Hoyt exited his Duster as Denny stormed past him.

"You okay, man?" Hoyt puzzled.

"You don't wanna know, Hoyt," Denny huffed as he unlocked his Roadrunner. "You *do not* wanna know."

* * * * * *

In the stillness of a moonless night, a gentle spring breeze rustled a swirl of dust across a freshly paved highway construction area under the glow of an isolated lamppost. Off in the distance, two approaching headlights danced about in the dark as a vehicle navigated the still ungraded section of the new road.

Arriving at the lone streetlight, Lucas Fischer's Dodge Challenger glistened purple diamonds against the night sky. Luke revved the 440 cubic inch engine for a few seconds, then let it resume idle as he exited the car and slowly sauntered around it in a counterclockwise inspection. Satisfied with his review, he was promptly back in the saddle – locked and loaded.

Luke reached down to a switch marked "line lock" and flipped it on – a dim red light indicated that the Challenger's front wheels were now seized until further notice. He then depressed the clutch and shifted his way through a mock gear-shifting exercise – complete with verbal sound effects.

"Rowrrrrrrrrr….Rerrrrrrrrr….Rurrrrrrrrr…..RAAAArrrrrer!"

Seventeen-year-old Luke was *playing drag race* in his mind the same way he did as a 9-year old with his toy Matchbox Ford Thunderbolt. But this beast was no toy.

Satisfied with his run through, Luke revved the 500+ horses of his 440 six-pack and wound it up to red line. Bringing it back to idle, Luke pulled his lap belt across and latched it to its base. Pushing the pistol grip gearshift into first, Luke took a deep breath and began to ramp-up the RPMs. As the tachometer reached 3,000, Luke popped the clutch… *unleashing holy Hell.*

As the rear tires broke their grip and began spinning wildly, Luke felt the back of the Challenger begin to hop left, then right again. Adrenaline pulsed through his veins like a sump pump on steroids, while thick, white smoke poured from the back wheel wells as if the rear end had suddenly gone aflame. Luke gripped the wheel tightly with his left hand as he reached down to the line lock switch and flipped the toggle off. The Challenger lunged forward like an attacking shark.

Luke's head was whipped back against the headrest – his neck failing to support the applied g-forces. He let out a yelp at the sudden, albeit slight, concussion of his head impacting the back of the seat. The Challenger roared like Godzilla ripping its way out of a giant cage. Luke's eyes bulged as he began to realize the impressive results of Hoyt's handy work.

"Hole-eeee shit!" Luke screamed as he slammed second gear and felt the torque break the rear wheels free again – leaving an 8-foot trail of black rubber upon the fresh pavement.

A smile was pasted across Luke's face as the RPMs climbed again. He prepared himself for the shift to third gear and banged the pistol grip forward. Luke had mistimed his clutch pump. The gears ground loudly as the engine screamed up well beyond 6,000 RPM. Luke was forced to lift his right foot, but only momentarily.

"Oh shit!" Luke yelled as he reapplied the clutch and slid the shifter into third.

The coasting vehicle was quickly up and running again. Luke cranked his third-gear RPMs up to 4,000 before he successfully slammed it hard into fourth. As he shifted, his eye caught the speedometer: 97 MPH. The rest was all gravy for Luke; he knew that every revolution gained meant even more top end.

"Yee-haw!" he yelled, "One-hundred and thirty *freakin'* miles-per-hour!"

Luke's celebration was short-lived however. Upon reaching this pinnacle, he'd lifted his foot off – rather than easing-up on the gas pedal. This caused an abrupt drop in RPMs. The ensuing loss of torque caused the rear tires to momentarily lock. Suddenly, Luke found himself in a tailspin. His rear end was chattering and sliding left-to-right. Because Luke had tried to steer out of the skid, rather than with it, the Challenger broke into a spin and headed – at 110 miles per hour – into a nearby meadow. Gobs of sod and muck were tossed skyward onto the hood and roof of Luke's once-purple gem. Luke gave up trying to steer and just stood on the brakes – hoping for the best result of this harrowing ride. The Challenger passed through a large section of freshly melted slush, water and grass, which splashed inside the hood onto the firewall-mounted voltage regulator – stalling the engine.

The car came to rest in 4-inches of muddy water. Luckily, only Luke's pride was damaged. He pulled hard for a deep breath, restarted the car, slid the gear knob into first and slowly fishtailed out of the soggy grass.

* * * * * * *

The familiar blast from a set of air horns, followed by the squeal of spinning tires announced the boisterous arrival of Steve Muller and his '67 Dodge Coronet R/T 426 Hemi. Hamming it up on the strip in front of Big Boy's Burgers and blasting his horn was Muller's trademark. Steve was proud of the fact that his 426 Hemi Coronet was "one of only 238 manufactured by Dodge in '67." With twin Carter 4-barrel carbs, the Coronet pushed 425 ponies right off the showroom floor, but Muller was better known for playing it safe, and as such, he often lost street duels when he lost his nerve.

Muller swung his monster Dodge into Big Boy's, while keeping a tiny bit of pressure on his gas pedal. The extra revs created a pop sound from his exhaust that nobody, save for the hearing impaired, could possibly ignore.

At the other end of the lot, consummate nerds, Harold and Barry made their first spring appearance, this time in a newer '70 Ford Maverick. With their matching horn-rimmed glasses and Brylcreem-slicked hair, Harold and Barry were muscle car wannabes, but looked a lot more like M.I.T. washouts.

Harold liked to brag that his Maverick had the optional, *Thriftpower Six*, 250-cid straight six engine. He'd tricked out the car with air shocks, baby moons and fuzzy dice. The boys were *cruisin' for chicks* in celebration of Harold's new ceramic skull shifter knob, which was freshly mounted on the column shift lever.

Sliding into a parking spot, the boys exited the Maverick. Harold leaned in and used his sleeve to wipe a speck of dust from the olive drab paint job. As they headed inside for burgers, one of the plastic air tubes that ran to the rear air shocks suddenly sprung from its bumper fitting. The car let loose with a loud hiss. The hose swung like a fish on a line, blasting out compressed air as the rear end sank, leaving the rear wheel wells sitting atop the tires. With this, the entire gang of motorheads in the parking lot broke into uproarious laughter. But Harold and Barry were safely inside, oblivious to the damage to the car… or their pride.

Mixed into the roar of laughter was the sound of a tri-powered 1965 GTO with a well-worked and bobcatted 428 engine. Tucker maneuvered the red Goat into one of the last remaining spots at the far end of the lot and exited quickly. He was late and knew how bitchy Hoyt could get when his stomach was grumbling.

As Tucker strutted quickly across the blacktop, he abruptly froze on the spot. From the midst of Woodward Avenue's bustling traffic emerged a black 1969 Mustang Boss 429. Tucker shook his head back into reality and let out a sigh as he saw Quentin Seymour cruise by in the Mustang's driver seat.

"Oh, thank God," Tucker breathed.

Quentin parked the Boss 429 next to Tucker's GTO and also headed for the diner.

Unbeknownst to Tucker, Hoyt, Denny or even Quentin, a shiny red '66 Ford Galaxie 500 convertible cruised slowly by Big Boy's, passed the entry and stopped at the set of lights on Woodward Avenue. Inside the Ford, Dawn peered over and spied Tucker as he headed inside to meet Hoyt.

Dawn's friend, Bernice – riding shotgun – shook her head in disgust. "I say screw him!" Bernice blurted out. "You obviously can't trust him."

Dawn bit her lip then drove away as the light turned green.

CHAPTER 7

Unbridled Attacks of Arrogance

Lucas Fisher weaved his car in and out of traffic along Woodward Avenue. He craned his neck while maneuvering past the slower cars. Up ahead, a fire-breathing Chevy Nova SS was rumbling vibration down into the pavement from its 396 cubes. Luke was attempting to get with the driver by the next light and issue a challenge. He doubted the Chevy could beat him, but Chevy guys always believed their cars could beat anything and Luke was banking on that fact.

As luck would have it, the driver in front of Luke signaled into the far left lane for a turn, giving the Challenger an open shot to the next light. Luke pulled even with the vibrating Nova. A small chrome scoop protruded from the hood of the Chevy.

"What's that, a '68?" Luke yelled over the din of the idling V-8 engines. "Sounds good."

The driver looked at Luke for a moment then looked away.

"Hey, mister!" Luke tried again. " Are you listening?"

The driver took a drag from his cigarette. "Look, kid, I'm not interested. Okay?"

Luke smirked arrogantly. "I wouldn't be either if I was driving that rat."

The driver shot Luke and angry stare then shook his head.

"Go away, son. You're bothering me."

Luke, showing his lack of street racing protocol, began his usual routine of intimidation – a chicken call – the same act that got him chased from Gratiot Avenue by a growing number of angry gearheads.

"Bock, bock, bock, baaaaahk!" Luke mocked.

It wasn't the actual chicken call that got to the driver, but Luke's arrogant smirk that really pissed him off. He revved the 440 up and held it at 2,500 RPM. The agitated Nova driver became red in the face and glared at Luke. This would not be what one would call "a friendly wager."

"Fifty bucks," the driver called over.

"This light!" Luke answered.

"Screw you, you little moron!" the driver responded. "You don't race on Woodward unless you want Boggs crawlin' up your ass!"

Luke knew he was about to race a seasoned street racer. This excited him, but was also slightly terrifying; just the way he liked it.

"Where to then?" Luke asked.

"Go west on 12 Mile," the driver said. "There's a new construction road on the left at Lathrup. You'll see it. Let's get this done."

The cars both revved up and peeled off at the green light, headed for battle.

* * * * * * *

Over the clinking of glasses, muffled jukebox music and the din of conversation inside Big Boy's, Tucker craned his neck in search of Hoyt and hopefully, Dawn. Hoyt emerged from the men's room, wiping his hands on a brown paper towel and immediately spotted Tucker. He motioned toward a booth and both maneuvered their way through the crowd. Sliding across from each other, Hoyt saw the immediate strain in Tucker's face.

"Do I have to ask?" Tucker shook his head.

"Nope. Not a sign of her at all," Hoyt answered with a dollop of sympathy.

"Shit."

Hoyt pasted a smile on. "Look Tuck," he said, "if it's any consolation, these things have a way of working themselves out. Anger fades, man."

Tucker wasn't convinced. "But it's the time in-between *mad* and *over it* when bad things can happen."

"What kind of bad?" Hoyt asked.

Tucker's eyes were drawn across the room to where the pretty blond, Alison, smiled as the arrogant goon, Kent Rager, was involved in a private conversation with Quentin Seymour.

"*Like that!*" Tucker exclaimed in total disbelief. "How can this be happening?"

"Like what?" Hoyt asked – confused by Tuckers' reference.

Hoyt stood up for a moment and gazed across at Rager. In doing so, his eyes met with Rager's. Rager whispered to Quentin, who also turned to look at Hoyt. A condescending smirk formed on Quentin's face as he spoke to Rager. Both kept their eyes pinned on Hoyt as they laughed together.

Hoyt quickly sat back down.

"Mother of God!" Hoyt exclaimed. "So that's what Denny meant! Man, I thought he was dead?"

"It can't be," Tucker shrugged and he attempted to peer through the jungle of bodies standing in the packed diner for another look.

Their confused state was broken by the arrival of Lenora.

"You guys want your usual?" she asked with a loud bubblegum pop added for emphasis.

"Yes, please" Hoyt answered.

"All three?" Lenora asked.

"No. Just two orders tonight, thanks." Tucker answered.

"Uh-oh," Lenore rolled her eyes as she turned away.

"So now what?" Hoyt whispered. "I'm gonna take a wild guess and claim that Rager ain't done with us yet."

"Screw him," Tucker said. "If he does want to race, he's got me living in his head already."

"Good evening, Moe and Larry," Rager was suddenly standing over them, propped on a scrolled wooden cane. "Where's little Shempette tonight?"

"Funny, Rager." Hoyt responded. "Where are your two trained chimps?"

"Oh, they're right outside," Rager smiled arrogantly. "They're checking out my new ride. Oh, it's much nicer than the last one. This one eats Goats and shits them out the tailpipe."

"Speaking of which," Tucker interjected. "You owe me a car."

"And you owe some slopes some new babies after you snuffed 'em out in Wun Phuc Yu," Rager grinned defiantly while Quentin snickered behind him.

"Why don't you take a hike, Rager?" Hoyt barked. "We thought you were dead. Too bad *that* didn't happen."

"You chumps can't burn me down like some Vietnamese village," Rager laughed arrogantly. "And I'm gonna reclaim what's rightfully mine."

Tucker stood and raised a fist, grabbing Rager by the lapel of his black leather coat. But he held off punching him. He released his grip on Rager.

"You're not worth the effort," Tucker sneered. "And I didn't hurt a soul in 'Nam that didn't try n' kill me first."

"That's what they all say," Rager scoffed.

Rager turned and motioned to Alison, who collected her hemp bag and car keys and scurried to catch up to Rager and Quentin. Rager turned back and motioned to Hoyt.

"When I beat that rolling boat anchor 340 out there, it'll be perfectly at home at the bottom of the Detroit River," Rager mocked. "There won't be another resurrection."

Hoyt jumped from his seat, but was held back by a few gearheads who'd been observing the confrontation.

"C'mon man," one of them said. "Can't you see the dude's on a cane?"

Rager leered back at Hoyt.

"That's right," Rager chuckled as he raised his cane up, "you shouldn't hit a cripple."

With a slight limp, Rager exited with Quentin and Alison to the parking lot.

The newly plotted subdivision off Lathrup had a brand new road, streetlights and drainage grids,. It was the perfect spot for a drag race. One morning a wide white stripe had appeared across the entry road. The construction crews knew what that meant; on any given night a drag race would begin on that stripe. Until the homes were built it would become a place the local police would probably ignore.

Tonight, Lucas Fischer's Challenger was sitting at that white line and was cranking some major horsepower through its massaged 440 engine while a few short feet away, the driver of a 1968 Nova Super Sport 396 was echoing the same.

With nobody to start the race, the two cars reversed back about 50 yards. From there, they would cruise, side-by-side, and return to the line, then stomp their pedals down in a rolling start drag race. The first car to reach the crosswalk at the next intersection would win. The finish line was a little more than a third-mile away.

With a nod, both drivers accelerated to 25 miles per hour and stayed even until they hit the line. At that point, both cars went into a wild, but short period of mayhem as menacing torque ripped rubber loose from the pavement. With wild fishtailing, the cars tore away from the line, finally grabbing the tar with melting tires as they sped off into the darkness.

In less than twenty-seconds, the cars had crossed the line – with the purple Challenger ahead by a full car length. The Nova's driver pulled up to Luke and handed him a wad of bills.

"Pleasure doing business with you," Luke grinned as he swiped the $50 from the driver's hand. "I hope you learned something tonight."

The driver glared at Luke. "Why you smug little bastard! I oughta…."

But before he could finish his sentence, Luke was gone in an instant. The Chevy driver could only hear Luke's condescending laughter over the grunt of his rumbling Challenger.

* * * * * * *

Denny took his very first bite of a *McDonald's* cheeseburger and then chased it with a large pinch of fries. He raised his eyebrows in surprised approval.

"This stuff ain't bad," he surmised as he pushed the cheeseburger back into his mouth. "Pretty good meal for fifty-two cents."

Denny looked over at his radio and winced as the *Five Stairsteps* came on.

> *O-o-Oh, Child, things are gonna get easier...*
> *O-o-Oh Child things'll get brighter...*

"Yeah right," Denny huffed as he punched the buttons on his radio until he settled on Sugarloaf's "Green-Eyed Lady."

To Denny's left, a red '66 Galaxie 500 slid into the open spot. Denny recognized Bernice and gave her a nod as he chewed on his burger. Behind the wheel, Dawn gave Denny a smile and a wave. Bernice rolled down the right side window.

"Hey, Den! What's happening?" Bernice asked with a coy smile.

Denny had pushed enough cheeseburger and fries into his mouth that he could barely choke out an answer.

"Hey 'Neese! Nuh mush. Hah buh you?"

Dawn leaned over her steering wheel and laughed, but her smile faded quickly.

"Mind if I eat with you?" She asked.

"Hey!" Bernice protested. "I'm sitting right here!"

"Just go inside, Bernie," Dawn said as she rolled her eyes. "I'll be right behind you. Besides this place is packed with single, hungry boys."

74

Bernice shrugged, nodded her head in agreement and exited the Galaxie.

Denny was confused, but sensed Dawn wanted his company. After his run-in with Rager, he could have used an ear as well.

Dawn and Denny had been friends since their days at Royal Oak High School. Dawn had shown some interest in Denny during their junior year when the Ravens' quarterback had been injured and Denny was moved from his halfback spot to starting QB. Abruptly, Denny had become the *big man on campus*. Dawn then "noticed" him and introduced herself. She was unaware that Denny had carried a torch for her since middle school, but when his chance to date her finally arrived, he was all-thumbs and had spat out a few pretty lame lines. Apparently, his nerves had gotten the better of him

Dawn was smart enough to see the nervousness that consumed Denny, but after two uncomfortable dates, they'd both decided to just remain *good friends*. Unlike many relationships that end *as friends*, Dawn and Denny had actually become close allies. They had a knack for running into each other whenever one of them hit an emotional wall and so it was tonight; when Dawn asked to join Denny, he knew she was experiencing some emotional chaos.

Or had she magically appeared because of Denny's problem with Alison and Rager?

Either way, both knew they'd feel a little bit better after taste-testing a few McDonald's burgers and crying on each other's shoulders.

By the time Dawn had reappeared with her bag of food, Denny had already completed his meal.

Inside, Bernice was getting flirty with a table full of hot rodders.

Denny decided to take a cruise up Woodward to the Loop while Dawn ate and he lamented about Rager and Alison. On their return trip, Dawn would take Tucker Knox's poor judgment to task.

Little were they aware that Steve Muller had spotted them in traffic and followed behind them while cruising in his '67 Coronet R/T. When Denny slid the Roadrunner back into a spot at McDonald's Dawn leaned over and gave her old friend Denny a peck on the check before exiting.

Witnessing this, Muller made a beeline for Big Boy's, where Tucker and Hoyt were probably hanging out in the parking lot.

* * * * * * *

Kent Rager slid a key into the ignition of his Boss 429 Mustang and sparked an explosion of sound and horsepower that resonated through Big Boy's parking lot. All heads turned as Rager eased up on the clutch pedal and engaged the massaged 429 brute forward and through the lot.

Tucker and Hoyt were emerging from Big Boy's as the Mustang lumbered by – its dual pipes cackling a whole lot of trouble for anyone who dared to even *think* about challenging it.

"Man, that thing *does* sound a heck of a lot more hairy than the last one," Hoyt groused as they watched the black monster roll onto the strip. "Hear that? That mill's been ported and re-carbed. You can actually hear it breathing!"

"Great," Tucker said sarcastically. "Just what I needed to hear tonight."

"Just don't race him for pinks, Tuck," Hoyt offered. "Keep it strictly for cash."

"No way." Tucker huffed. "He'll try to coerce me in front of a crowd. He'll put me on the spot to run for pinks."

Hoyt tried to reassure him. "I have some tricks up my sleeve. Just relax," he said.

The familiar air horn blast of Steve Muller's Coronet R/T reverberated from the avenue and precluded the rumbling arrival of his big Hemi. Muller drove in a direct line toward Tucker and Hoyt, then leaned out his window.

"Hey boys! Havin' a good night?" Muller was somewhat animated in his expression. A wide smile was pasted across his face.

Steve Muller was known as a *fun guy* to the other drivers, but not all that bright. The car bug had bitten him when he was just a freshman in high school and he'd quit school in order to work on cars. His mother wasn't too pleased, but his father – secretly proud that

Steve was following in his footsteps – took him into his small automotive repair shop and showed him the ropes.

"What's up, Stevie?" Hoyt asked.

"I'm wondering the same thing, man," Muller feigned seriousness. "I just seen that Dawn chick. She was cruisin' around with Denny in his Roadrunner."

Muller voiced this loud enough for Tucker to overhear, which caused Tucker to spin on his heels toward Muller.

"What are you selling?" Tucker demanded.

"I ain't sellin' nothing," Muller retorted, "I'm just sayin' I seen Denny cruisin' Woodward with that cute chick, Dawn riding shotgun. That's all I'm saying."

Tucker looked upward – swallowing hard on a chunk of bitter disappointment. "Really," he said as a-matter-of-factly. "That's pretty interesting."

Hoyt gave Tucker a nudge amplified with a boyish grin.

"Come on, man," he laughed. "Denny's cool. He's no hound dog. I've known him since that *Rare Earth* concert we went to in '68. He's been in Big Boy's a million times. He's a straight shooter."

Despite his extraordinarily thick skull, Muller sensed the tension in the air and attempted to smooth over his intentional bomb toss.

"Oh yeah, man," Muller chuckled. "Denny ain't nothin' to worry about."

Unconvinced, Tucker headed for his GTO, leaving Hoyt standing in the parking lot.

"That didn't go over too well," Muller mulled.

"Gee, Muller," Hoyt snapped, "You think so?"

Muller allowed Hoyt's response to settle into his feeble brain while mouth-breathing a few respiratory cycles before he realized Hoyt's sarcasm.

"Oh man," Muller responded, "I guess I should have shut up 'bout that, huh?"

CHAPTER 8

All is Lost… or is it?

Rager laughed and slapped the top of his steering wheel as he goosed the Boss 429 along Woodward Avenue. He had the windows down, allowing in the cool night air along with the inspiring sound of tuned resonation from his dual pipes puffing out horsepower. Duly impressed, Alison could only smile from ear-to-ear as the fresh air streamed through her long blond locks.

"This Boss is just *sooo bitchin'*, Alison laughed as Rager goosed the accelerator.

As Rager cruised and weaved through traffic, he could see pedestrians on either side of the road who would stop and turn to watch as the big, bad Mustang roared loudly past them. Some were annoyed – most were simply amazed. But one other person was closely observing Rager's progress along Woodward Avenue.

Luke Fischer was cruising five car-lengths behind Rager as they headed north on the strip. Luke was weighing-up his odds were he to issue a challenge to Rager. He had no idea who Rager was, or about Rager's sordid history of violent street duals or the death of Dwayne Macy, which Rager had caused by squeezing Macy's Z/28 off at a construction bottleneck. To the young Fischer kid, Rager was just another "older dude" – one whom he had to beat with his Challenger.

With youthful ignorance, Fischer decided that by utilizing simple mathematics he could predict the outcome of their drag race. The Challenger had 440 cubic inches under the hood.

"The most that Ford can have under the hood would be a 429," Luke reasoned. "That gives me an eleven-cubic inch advantage. And since my rear tires are fatter, I'll have better grip!"

What Lucas Fischer Jr. did not reckon with was the fact that Rager had several years of experience on him, as well as a car that weighed a little more than 300 pounds less than his Challenger.

Those *eleven cubes* stuck in Luke's head like oatmeal tossed against a wall, as he stomped the Dodge's accelerator and steered his way through traffic to catch up with the Boss 429. Up ahead, the lights went yellow at an intersection. Luke put his foot deeper into the gas and zoomed ahead in order to meet Rager at the red. The Challenger swung onto the shoulder and rounded one last vehicle before cutting-off the driver and speeding to a stop: right next door to Rager's idling 429 beast.

Rager took a quick glance at the purple Challenger then chuckled when he saw its young driver. Focusing on the red light, Rager ignored Luke's deafening revs of the 440 six-pack.

"What's the matter?" Luke called over. "Chicken?"

Alison turned toward Rager as he snickered to himself – not giving Luke the satisfaction of a response.

"Hey! Leather jacket!" Luke tried again. "I'm talking to you, tough guy. Is that one of those *FORDS*? You know, *fix or repair daily*?" Luke chortled.

Rager rolled his eyes and decided to ignore the little monster.

"He could beat your ass in a heartbeat!" Alison responded.

"Don't." Rager whispered.

Luke kept up with his spiel; the same antagonizing drivel that had eventually caused him to be chased him off Gratiot Avenue when angry drivers had listened to enough of his tripe.

"So sad. I'll bet the only thing you'll be beatin' tonight is your *meat*, huh buddy?"

Rager felt his face become flush red. The kid had finally found the right stick to poke into Rager's ribs. He turned and shot Luke a stare that sent a cold chill down his spine.

"You don't have any idea who you're messing with do you? I normally don't race little boys," Rager quipped, "at least not until they've grown a few ball hairs."

"Ha–ha, you're pretty funny," Luke shot back. "Not bad for an old bastard."

"What's it gonna be, mamma's boy? One hundred? Five hundred?" Rager's face remained stone cold.

Luke dug into his pants pocket and pulled out a wad of bills.

"Yeah man, a hundred sounds good," he said assertively. "Do you want to head north?"

Rager laughed aloud. "No punk. You're not getting off that easy. We're going back to Big Boy's to roust up some additional action on this. I can drop off my girl at her car. Then we're heading north to Baldwin. That's where I'll be taking daddy's hard-earned cash."

"I'm his girl!" Alison flashed as she wiggled closer to Rager and snuggled his right arm.

* * * * * * *

Tucker was headed south after cruising though the McDonald's parking lot. He'd seen neither Dawn's nor Denny's vehicles, which didn't make him feel any better about Muller's revelation.

He downshifted the GTO and gave the 428 cubes a steady application of pedal – just enough to make the pipes gurgle in resonant harmony. Abruptly, he spied Denny's bright orange Roadrunner up ahead. Tucker pushed the pedal down and downshifted again, causing a light chirp from the rear tires as he sped toward Denny.

Denny was bopping to a *Three Dog Night* tune on his radio as he cruised along with all windows lowered. Tucker pulled the GTO along side and yelled over to Denny, who was startled enough to jam his brakes for a moment.

"Hey Denny, what's happening?" Tucker feigned a lack of concern. He kept the GTO even with the door frames of the Roadrunner.

Denny expression immediately betrayed him – like the cat who'd just swallowed the canary.

"Oh... uh... hi there, Tuck," he said sheepishly. "What's up with you? How's the goat running?"

Tucker's expression left no doubt about his frustration.

Denny decided not to play the game. "Look man," he pleaded, "She came to me. We're old friends. We got some chow and she told me her problems with you. That's all."

"Problems?" Tucker asked. "You mean there's more than one?"

"You know what I mean, Tucker." Denny struggled to stay above the whirlpool that threatened to suck him down into Tucker's swirling emotions. "We've been friends for years, Tucker. You don't need to worry about this."

Tucker shrugged, "Yeah, I know. I heard. So where'd she go?"

"As far as I know, she went home for the night," Denny offered.

"Thanks, man." Tucker replied. "Didn't mean to hassle you, brother."

Both drivers swung to the turn around and cruised back toward Big Boy's parking lot, where a gigantic cluster of gearheads and groupies were gathered in the lot.

Tucker and Denny parked and shook hands, then headed to see what the commotion was about. It didn't take long for them to see who the ringleader was, as Kent Rager stood on his doorsill and preached to the crowd with as much drama as a television evangelist.

"Okay, my fine friends!" Rager proclaimed. "As you can see, it's kiddie toy night and this fine young, well… whatever he is, has issued me a *challenge*!"

Rager pointed a menacing finger at young Lucas Fischer. The crowd let out an approving cheer.

"He seems to think this… this…. goofy-grape-looking farm tractor has a chance at beating me and my trusty steed. That is, my 500 horsepower steed."

The crowd laughed and cheered again. None seemed to question how or why Rager was still alive, still racing and still pissing-off almost every person he dealt with.

Stan stepped forward on Rager's queue. "Okay people! Place your bets! Get 'em in while you still can!" he bellowed.

As they collected bets, Ralph helped Stan by jotting down names on a small note pad.
Tucker spotted Hoyt as he emerged from the swirling pool of bettors.

"Don't tell me you punted a bet with those morons," Tucker laughed.

"Why not?" Hoyt shrugged. "I'm always gonna bet on my own work. The kid might be green, but that Challenger is boasting some major testosterone!"

"Cane or no cane, I've raced Kent Rager and I'd never bet against him," Tucker shot back. "I'll take unbridled insanity over pure grunt in this scenario."

"I think they're both assholes," Denny offered.

A mass exodus followed, as the gearheads and groupies scurried for their vehicles and streamed out of Big Boys – all headed for Baldwin Avenue.

Hoyt climbed into Tucker's GTO as Denny jogged off for his Roadrunner.

"Rager's not as badass as he was in the old days," Hoyt laughed. "Driving all the way past the Pontiac Loop just to avoid any heat? That's nuts, man!"

Tucker, still lost in his concern over Dawn, looked at it from a more negative perspective.

"If Rager hurts this kid, or if he flips his Mopar and kills himself, that'll be the end of Dawn and me," he moped. "We should have left his car outside."

"And close our business for good?" Hoyt seethed. "Look, we're in the speed business, Tuck. Dawn knows that. She shouldn't be road-blocking customers on us."

"Let's see how the kid handles all those new ponies you've bolted under that hood," Tucker said. "If he survives – hell if he *beats* Rager – maybe Dawn will cool off."

The area was being prepped for a new subdivision, but only a model home stood at the entrance. The UAW strike had stopped most of the new construction over most of Lower Michigan.

Tucker's GTO swung down the newly-paved road in a dense haze of white powdery dust created by the dozens of cars that were arriving to watch the Ford vs. Mopar duel.

Word traveled quickly whenever a major duel was about to go down and tonight was no exception. Dozens of cars were streaming in to watch Kent Rager's first comeback race against the *new kid in town* that had the strip all abuzz..

As was customary, the two contestants arrived fashionably late for maximum dramatic effect. This also boosted the betting action as everyone had a second chance to size-up the beef before the starting light flashed. All that was missing tonight was a hot dog and beer vendor.

As the last car parked and shutdown its engine, the area fell into an eerie silence. Most of the crowd only spoke in low tones – avoiding any chance of the locals dialing-up the Pontiac police department.

Abruptly, the distant rumbling of well-massaged, all-American cast iron V-8 engines dashed the silence as they approached Baldwin Avenue. As the sound grew louder, so did the suppressed excitement; this race was going to be a nasty one. As expected, Rager was first on the scene. He still had trouble climbing upon his door windowsill to address his audience, so Stan emptied an old milk crate full of greasy tools into the trunk of his '66 Chevelle SS and flipped it over for Rager to use as a step.

Slowly flipping open his official "NASA Moon Landing" Zippo lighter, Rager ignited the flame and lit a Lucky Strike. He dragged slowly, as if in deep thought, before addressing his fans.

"So here we are again," Rager spoke as he slowly surveyed the masses. "The return of the king – the *Comeback Kid*, if you will."

Stan and Ralph began to whistle and clap, but immediately stopped when Rager raised his palm to them.

"There's been a lot of talk about this new kid in town, how he's arrogant and a loose cannon. But I'm not concerned about that, because I see a lot of myself in this kid," Rager continued. "He's got the hardware and the cocky attitude – just like me. Unfortunately, I'm gonna have to take him down a notch, so this race ain't for pinks. It's for cash and a cautionary tale for our little friend, Luke… Luke the Puke."

Stan and Ralph broke out again in laughter and whistling at Rager's pun, which signaled the rest of the crowd to follow suit. The cheering grew louder as Rager pumped a leather-gloved fist into the air, but seconds later the cheering was buried under the sound of the approaching Challenger.

The inexperienced Lucas Fischer didn't know nor care that the proper and dramatic way to enter a dual was slow and loud. Instead, he zoomed-in fast – scaring people who were still in the road – then exited his car quickly. His lack of protocol turned all the attention from Rager over to Luke and that's exactly what Luke wanted.

"It's nice to see you all," Luke smirked. "My name is Lucas, but you can call me Luke. I'm here to knock this arrogant old grandpaw off his throne."

Ralph immediately charged at Lucas. "What do you mean by old?" Ralph barked. "Rage ain't even 30 yet! Right, Rage?"

Rager shrugged. Age was the least of his concerns, but Luke was using it as a weapon to talk smack.

"This is a young man's game now, ol' yeller tooth," Luke smirked. "We race to Led Zeppelin now – not Buddy freakin' Holly."

"Why, you little bastard!" Ralph yelled as he again attempted to attack Luke. "You ain't getting' away with insulting my boss!"

Rager raised his hand at Ralph again. "Let's do our fighting on the strip. Stan, get the C-note from Beaver Cleaver over there so we can get this ball rolling."

Stan retrieved Luke's ball of cash and counted it on the hood of his Chevelle as Ralph dug out a starter flashlight from the trunk.

"We race from here to the I-75 overpass," Rager announced. "It's a whole mile and then some, so any interruption by our friendly neighborhood pigs will automatically cancel the race till tomorrow night."

Luke shrugged it off. "You wanna go the distance instead of a quarter mile? That's fine with me," he said. " You'll lose no matter which way we race."

"You might wanna change that diaper before we start, little man," Rager quipped. "By the time I'm through with you and your grape mobile, you'll be packing those fancy chinos with enough shit to fertilize your mom's flower garden."

"You're pretty funny, Mr. Rager," Luke replied. "Did ya get that joke off the back of your Geritol bottle?"

"Get in your car," Rager shot back. "Keep your big mouth shut. You might learn something, wise guy."

Luke skipped back to his Mopar while Rager sparked the Boss to life. When Luke's Challenger started, the sound of both cars overwhelmed the night air with a thunderous rumble.

The crowd moved back and away as the cars inched forward toward the painted white line in the street. Ralph scurried between the two cars, then spun to face them as he raised his flashlight.

"Tach 'em up and burn!" Ralph yelled.

At that, both cars roared forward at full throttle, burning rubber off the rear tires. Thick white smoke enveloped them as they slowly backed their cars to the starting line.

"I love that smell," Hoyt yelled.

The crowd of spectators laughed loudly, causing Hoyt to withdraw back into his shell – his face flushed red.

Ralph raised the flashlight again as both cars revved-up. This time, they were standing on their brakes. Luke had his line-lock activated and allowed his rear tires to spin. Both cars growled like tortured lions on steroids as they bounced from the sheer power being transferred to their rear axles.

At the flash of Ralph's light, both cars launched like lightning across the line and past the amazed queue of spectators.

The race was on.

CHAPTER 9

Resolution

D awn brushed her hair as she stared into her vanity mirror. Noticeably upset, she dabbed a crumpled tissue beneath one eye as she took a deep breath. Part of her wanted to run to her car and speed to Big Boy's, while her more stubborn side was telling her that she had every right to be pissed-off. She reached to her vanity a grabbed an open can of beer. She paused once more to look at herself before putting the can to her lips.

"This oughta solve everything," she said as she raised the can in a toast to the mirror. "Here's to not always being right about everything!"

Dawn chugged down the entire can and wiped her lips with the tissue. She then fired the tissue against the mirror. It stuck to the pane, directly over the reflection of her mouth, causing Dawn to burst out in laughter.

"That's the answer," she laughed. "I'll just stuff my mouth with Kleenex and everyone will get along just fine!"

Dawn stood, threw back her hair, and then pulled on a tasseled leather jacket over a faded brown *Mitch Ryder and the Detroit Wheels* t-shirt. She grabbed her keys and headed for the door.

* * * * * * *

As Kent Rager and Lucas Fischer blasted away from the starting line, Tucker turned and looked away. He scanned the crowd, hoping to see Dawn, attempting to lose herself among the rowdy spectators. Hoyt caught Tucker's desperation and shoved an elbow into his side.

"Hey dude, there's a race happening! Get your head in the game, man," Hoyt chuckled – trying not to sound too serious.

Tucker looked back at Hoyt and then feigned interest in the drag race. "Yeah, yeah… I'm back," he snipped.

Already one hundred yards off the line, Rager grinned as he slammed the Boss Mustang into third gear. He could barely see the left rear corner of Luke Fischer's Challenger in his rear view mirror, but that was enough to let him know that Fischer was behind by a few feet. Rager's smooth transition from 2nd to 3rd gear jumped the Boss ahead a little more, but Lucas was still winding out 2nd gear a bit more before mashing a shift to 3rd, which suddenly put him even with Rager.

The high-horsepower monsters wrestled back and forth within inches of the lead as the RPMs wound toward the 4th gear shifting point. Rager pulled back hard into 4th – perhaps somewhat prematurely – and felt his 429 bog ever so slightly. This missed shift gave Luke a half car length lead.

"Woooo-hoooo!" Luke screamed, realizing he had plenty of pedal left and still had a final shift into 4th to boost him forward.

Rager remained calm, but questioned his new Mustang's ferocity in the face of a true challenge.

C'mon now, Quentin, you bastard! Where are the ponies?" Rager yelled out, "This is what I pay you for!"

For Luke, watching his tach click-off the final few hundred RPMs before shifting felt like an eternity, but when the time came, his mind flashed back to the previous night's mishap and lubricated slide through the muddy sod. This time, there would be no missing 4th gear.

Luke held off until the RPMs hit 3,000 and pulled hard on the pistol-grip shift knob.

"Yes!" Luke bellowed out as the Challenger transitioned smoothly into 4th.

Rager's headlights were now a few feet behind the Challenger. In his own headlights, Luke spotted the I-75 overpass; he only had a quarter-mile at best before he could claim victory!

Rager remained strangely cool and collected. He saw the Challenger bump ahead slightly as Luke shifted into 4th gear, but he also knew that he was gaining back territory. If he could only close the gap in the few hundred yards that remained before they passed under the bridge.

Rather than fighting the headwind, Rager jumped-in behind the Challenger, using it to draft himself within an inch or two of Luke's bumper. The thought crossed Rager's mind to bump the kid and put him into a spin, but even Kent Rager wouldn't put a teenager's life in jeopardy. Instead, Rager peered to the side; he had to time his jump perfectly in order to slingshot himself past Luke before the overpass. Do this too soon, and Lucas could run past him again.

"Hold it. Hold it..." Rager studied the approaching bridge. "NOW!"

Rager swung the Boss 429 out to the left and accelerated past the Challenger. He realized that he had gained an inch of gas pedal while drafting, so he stomped it down. The Ford moved ahead of the growling Dodge! As the two cars reached the overpass, Luke had closed the gap, but the distance had run its course.

Rager had won by less than a car length.

The cars screeched to a rapid stop and both drivers exited. Neither seemed happy.

"I had you! I had you old man," Luke was red-faced and he screamed. "You know I had you!"

Rager stared coldly at Luke, "I beat you through sheer experience, punk," he said. "You don't mess with the king. You'll lose every time."

"King? Ha!" Luke laughed. "You got lucky!"

"Luck had nothing to do with it, zit face," Rager scoffed. "Now beat feet back to daddy, little boy. I've got places I gotta be."

"No way you won!" Luke protested. "You cheated!"

"And I did that how?"

"You... you changed lanes. That's NASCAR crap!" Luke blurted. "You can't draft in drag racing!"

"All I know is we bet on who would make it to the overpass first. That happened to be me," Rager answered. "So I'll be taking your deposit or my boys will take it in parts off that pukey-plum thing you call a ride." Luke looked behind him to see Stan's tattered '66 Chevelle SS arriving. He quickly dug cash out of his jeans pocket.

"Fine!" Luke shrugged as he steamed at Rager. "But this ain't over!"

"In a way, you're right," Rager nodded. "Because from now on, you'll be driving for me."

"What?" Luke blurted.

Rager belched an evil laugh as Luke bristled at the mention of being one of Rager's thugs.

'I want you to join my little club," Rager was suddenly serious. "I can set up plenty of street action for you – for a percentage, of course."

Luke stepped toward Rager, his face knotted in bewilderment.

"What do you mean by *set-up*?" he frowned. "And what kind of percentage are you talking here?"

Stan and Ralph were suddenly behind Lucas; close enough for Lucas to smell their nicotine and beer-laced breath. Ralph chuckled as he lit his 50th *Lucky Strike* of the day.

Rager offered Luke a cigarette, which was waved off.

"Look, kid, you can cruise Woodward Avenue every night looking for strokes to challenge, but eventually you'll run out of luck when the pigs catch on or some pissed-off loser hands you a beating because you ripped the ass off his beloved Camaro. You've got talent, kid. All you need is a good manager to set up some money runs and some muscle behind you to keep the goons from stuffing that fifty-dollar haircut up your tailpipe."

Luke ran his hand through his hair.

"So let's talk turkey. How much is your take?"

Rager paused to exhale a plume of cigarette smoke. "I'm bank. I'm putting the cash on the line. All you have to do is win; you and that purple blob you're driving. When you win, you take twenty-five percent and the bank – meaning me – takes the rest."

"Are you kidding me?" Luke recoiled again. "That's bullshit, man!"

Rager kept his cool and grinned as Lucas continued his fit by storming off to his Challenger, opening the door, slamming it shut again and stomping back to Rager.

"When you're racing for a thousand bucks, a two-hundred and fifty dollar take ain't too bad when you can't lose a penny," offered Rager. "I can set these races up and you can rake-in the wins and the profits. Unless, of course, you wanna just keep racing for chump change."

"Why don't you do the racing then?" Luke grimaced.

"I got lots of irons in other fires," Rager answered. " I'm lucky if I can run twice a week."

"Well why don't your two flunkies race for you?" Luke puzzled as he watched Stan picking his nose.

"Those two couldn't run a lemonade stand without finding a way to get themselves locked-up by Boggs," Rager spit as he nodded toward Stan.

Ralph took exception to Rager's depiction. "Hey, Rage, that ain't exactly right, I think you...." Ralph was quickly headed-off.

"You don't get paid to think, Ralph!" Rager hissed.

Stan laughed at Ralph as he wiped a booger on his shirt.

"These morons get paid to do other jobs for me," Rager explained. "I need a reliable driver – someone with half a brain, who I can trust to be where they're supposed to be and knock out the competition."

"So I put up no cash and if I win I get twenty-five percent of the take?" Luke asked.

"Right."

"And what happens if I lose? Let's say I lose three out of five?" Luke mulled.

"We'll just make some corrections," Rager answered.

"Oh yeah, sure! What kind of corrections, Mr. Rager?" Luke winced. "Like a physical beating?"

Rager rubbed his chin and took another drag from his cigarette.

"No. We'll have my mechanic look at your wheels and try to figure out where we can add some extra grunt," Rager assured him. "I need you to drive. I don't make any money if you're in a hospital bed."

Luke kicked some dirt around with his toe. "When do I start?"

"Friday night. Big Boys. Eight o'clock," Rager said. "It's a half-a-G-note runoff with a Buick GS. Don't be late and don't stiff me."

"I'll be there!" Luke laughed don't you worry about that!'"

* * * * * * *

The cars were just rolling back into Big Boys as Dawn exited her Galaxie 500. Realizing she'd just missed a major street duel, she stopped to watch the parade of muscle cars arriving. She spied Denny's Roadrunner pulling in and walked over as he parked his Mopar.

"Hey Den, where was the race?" Dawn asked as Denny stepped from his Plymouth.

"It was up at Baldwin," Denny related. "Kent Rager beat that new punk in his purple Challenger."

"Do you mean, Lucas Fischer?" Dawn asked.

"Yeah, that kid," Denny laughed. "Rager beat him and claims he's the new king of Woodward Ave."

"Gee, that doesn't sound like Kent Rager at all," Dawn said as she rolled her eyes.

"You here to find Tucker?" Denny asked.

Dawn sighed. "Yeah, we need to talk. I understand the business he's in. I just need to come to terms with what guys do with their big, bad cars."

"You've seen the light, Dawn! Congrats!" Denny laughed.

"Yes, the blinding light of burning Detroit steel, crumpled on the side of some remote country road," she joked.

"Aw, c'mon Dawn," Denny winked. "It ain't that bad."

"Really? Tell that to your insurance company," Dawn smirked. "Wanna go in and grab a Coke?"

Denny and Dawn disappeared into the throng of gearheads filing into Big Boys just as Hoyt and Tucker arrived in Hoyt's 340 Duster. Tucker was already scanning the lot for Dawn's red Ford Galaxie as the Duster turned in.

"Don't worry, Tuck, she'll be here," Hoyt assured Tucker. "You guys have some kind of *radar love* thing goin' on!"

"Radar love thing?" Tucker chuckled.

"Hey! That would make a great song, don't you think?" Hoyt laughed. "*Radar Love*. Wow!"

"Never happen, Willie," Tucker speculated. "That just sounds foolish."

Inside Big Boys, Lenora had her hands full as she juggled her tables with a few additional booths that the new help couldn't handle. It was all old hat to Lenora – she was well aware that a post-race crowd always showed-up hungry and full of exciting news from the streets.

Having arrived slightly early, Denny and Dawn had a prime location: a booth at the front window. Lenora took their order and moved on to cool down a table full of bickering Mustang and Z/28 gearheads.

It didn't take long for Dawn's own inner *radar love* app to focus in on Tucker's impending arrival. She spied him as he crossed the parking lot with Hoyt.

"Oh, boy," Dawn whispered, but loud enough for Denny to overhear.

"Ah! King Tuck as arrived!" Denny laughed. "Fireworks time?"

"No, no," Dawn shook her head. "Reconciliation time. Hopefully with some compromise."

"You'll do fine," Denny offered.

"You're a good friend, Denny," Dawn grinned.

"I'm gonna make myself scarce," Denny said. "Tell Lenora I moved over to eat with the Mopar Mob."

Within seconds after Denny cleared out, Hoyt was standing over Dawn's booth. "Eating alone tonight?" Hoyt joked.

"I certainly hope not, William. Have a seat?"

Hoyt slid in across from Dawn. As quickly as he did, awkwardness suddenly took over the meeting.

"No Tucker tonight?" Dawn prodded, knowing Tucker was there. Somewhere.

"Oh, he saw your car in the lot," Hoyt nodded. "I'm sure he's checking his hair in the boy's room."

"Got room for one more?" Tucker asked as quickly as he appeared from the crowd surrounding the booths. Dawn simply nodded without making too much eye contact. Tucker slid in next to Hoyt – directly across from Dawn.

"Oh, really, Tuck?" Dawn rolled her eyes at his social ineptitude.

"Oh...uh, sorry." Tucker scrambled to his feet and slid in next to Dawn.

"Hi!" she said.

Tucker nodded. "Hi, Hon."

96

"Well!" Hoyt blurted. "Looks like I can go hang with Denny and the Roadrunners!"

"Don't you dare!" Dawn objected. "This has just as much to do with you as it does with Tucker!"

"Uh, okay," Hoyt whimpered.

"Look, can we get this right out on the table and work it out?" Dawn pleaded. "I don't like feeling like this. I'm not the authority on this. I just have strong feelings about it."

"Then what are we going to do about it?" Tucker asked.

"Yeah... what he said," Hoyt echoed.

"We have to do what we do, Dawn," Tucker offered. "Our business depends on it. I have an idea though...."

"And what is that?" Dawn asked.

"With every invoice for every car we work on and in our shop, we can be advocates for safe, organized track racing," Tucker explained. "We can push our customers to consider running at Detroit Dragway.... or Milan or anywhere but the street."

"We could ask them to sign a waiver saying they'll at least *try* organized racing," Hoyt added. "Maybe they'll get a taste of the quarter-mile strip and start racing there on weekends."

Dawn pondered their offer for a few moments, before shaking her head.

"You know?" she said, "That just might work. It could get street racing out of their numb skulls. What a great idea! But one more thing...."

"What?" Hoyt and Tucker asked simultaneously.

"Never talk about the cars you work on while you're with me?" Dawn added. "I mean, you can talk about them, but I don't want to know what cars they are or who owns them. I'd rather not know. Just do your best to keep your customers safe?"

"That could be our new slogan," Tucker said. "Making you fast – keeping you safe."

"Perfect!" Hoyt agreed.

"I like that too, Tuck," Dawn grinned.

Hoyt squirmed in his seat, Tucker and Dawn immediately knew he was about to go off on a rant, so they leaned back and let him run.
"We could go after the whole *handling the horsepower* idea," Hoyt explained. "A car with gobs of raw power needs great suspension to handle all that juice! We could put in stiffer shocks and springs, anti-roll bars and punch up the wheel diameters and tread width. Hell, we could even lower the suspension slightly to give the car a lower center of gravity!"

"Sounds interesting…" Dawn injected.

"SHHH! I'm not done, Dawn!" Hoyt protested. "If we sell the idea of making our customers safe by building a "power plus suspension" package that keeps them on the road and out of the ditch, we'll have drivers beating down our doors from all over Michigan!"

"But…" Tucker butted-in.

"Wait! Not done." Hoyt pushed back. "I've been thinking about what Pontiac did to the Trans Am last year," Hoyt went on. "If we apply a spoiler on the rear deck or a wing like the Judge has, we can create down force that'll keep the rear tires on the road. The front of those Trans Ams have an air dam. If we could create custom air dams that just bolt on to the most popular super cars? Well, they'll push air *around* the car instead of snowplowing it! Fiberglass is the way to go.

We just make a cardboard template and hand it over to the hull repair dudes at the nearest marina." Yeah…. That would be a gas, man!"

Tucker paused for a moment. "Done?"

"Yeah, I'm done," Hoyt laughed.

Lenora arrived with Dawn's meal just as the threesome laughed.

"Well, it looks like everything is back to normal on Lover's Lane," Lenora teased. "You two guys want your usual?"

"You know it," Hoyt grinned.

Lenora moved off as Tucker put his arm around Dawn.

Dawn leaned into Tucker and sighed. "Well, that was a longest 24 hours of my life."

"I can relate," Tucker nodded.

"Me too!" Hoyt added as he grabbed a handful of Dawn's french fries from her plate. "Got my appetite back now."

CHAPTER 10

Rager's New Warrior

Quentin Seymour squinted into the engine compartment of the 1970 Challenger R/T. He moved his shoplight back and forth as he examined the few visible add-ons that Hoyt had installed on Lucas Fischer's Dodge. Kent Rager leaned on Quentin's shoulder, cigarette between his lips, and watched as Quentin worked.

"What do you see, Q?" Rager asked.

"Hmmm, that Hoyt is a sneaky little rodent," Quentin explained. "You never know what he's had his mitts on, know what I mean? I can bet he changed the carb jets and he probably didn't mess around with this six-pack intake too much, you know what I mean? I'm gonna guess he pulled the heads and put on thinner gaskets – probably polished up the ports too. Know what I mean?"

"Yeah, Q," Rager teased. "We know what you mean."

Rager turned to Luke, who was sitting back and letting Quentin do his inspection. "Hey kid, what exactly did Hoyt to your 440?" Rager asked.

"I'm not sure," Luke stammered. "I kinda just gave him 500 bucks and told him to give me more beef."

"Receipt?"

"Uh. No." Luke shook his head. "I tossed it out so my dad wouldn't find it."

"Brilliant." Rager spat out.

"If he paid him 500 clams, then Hoyt probably three-angled the valve seats, ported and polished the heads," Quentin offered. "Know what I mean?"

"Did you notice any more punch after Hoyt massaged it?" Rager asked Luke.

"Oh yeah! It was groovy, man! Thing just moved out!" Luke beamed.

"Heads." Rager nodded.

"Yep, heads," Quentin agreed. "We're gonna have to go inside, know what I mean?"

"Cam?" Rager asked.

"Yep, a cam," Quentin answered. "Headers n' pipes too."

"How do you know Hoyt didn't already replace the cam?" Luke asked.

"See them bolts on the water pump?" Quentin pointed at the engine. "Ain't been touched since day one at the Dodge assembly line. Hoyt made you go faster, but I can tell that boy has a good heart, because he didn't want a kid like you going too fast – know what I mean?"

"Yeah," Luke nodded. "I know exactly what you mean."

* * * * * * * *

Dawn maneuvered her '66 Galaxie 500 around a few trees and onto the grassy edge of the overlook. Beyond the hood, the lights of Detroit shimmered in the cool spring air. Dawn shut off the car and took a deep breath.

"This is why I got the convertible. Just look at those stars!" Dawn said as she slid across the seat close to Tucker. "This was where we had our first kiss, remember?"

"How could I forget?" Tucker laughed. "You attacked me."

"Oh, I did not!" Dawn laughed as she slapped Tucker's shoulder.

"Well, it certainly caught me by surprise," Tucker recalled. "I was wide-eyed and innocent.'

"Oh, right!" Dawn laughed. "A guy comes home from the war in Vietnam and he's afraid of lil' ol' me?"

"Hey, I hadn't really talked to a girl in over a year," he said. "I was freaking out about how I could ever get a kiss from you."

"So you never got a... you know, in Vietnam... a...." Dawn stammered.

"What, a hooker? Oh no!" Tucker laughed. "Are you kidding me? When I saw guys literally crying out because they said it felt like they were pissing glass, I had no intention of getting myself contaminated with that kind of exotic disease."

"Good for you!" Dawn smiled. "You were a good boy then."

"Yeah..." Tucker sighed. "Almost too good."

"So, do I have to make the first move again tonight?"

Tucker pulled Dawn tightly against him. "Probably not this time," he said as he kissed her softly, then with slightly more passion with each additional kiss.

Tucker ran his hand up Dawn's thigh. He was amazed at how perfectly smooth and soft her skin felt.

Despite his chiseled good looks, Tucker wasn't exactly a ladies man. He'd signed up for military service right out of high school and couldn't wait to get to Vietnam to discover the fate of his lost brother, Chris. It was all he was focused on. Women had slid pretty low on his list of priorities – that was until this moment.

Abruptly, Dawn stopped kissing him and pushed him back.

"I don't know if we're ready for this," she whispered.

"I don't know either," Tucker agreed.

"Oh hell, let's just do it then," Dawn answered as she grabbed Tucker's t-shirt and pulled it over his head.

In the distance, the dampened sounds of Detroit resonated in a symphony of roaring engines, car horns and the occasional squeal of burning rubber. All of that was beautiful background music to Tucker and Dawn as they wrestled with each others' clothing.

"*Oh my God...* Tucker," Dawn cried out – breaking the silence of the overlook for a brief moment.

* * * * * * *

Kent Rager rolled over and pulled a Lucky Strike from a crumpled pack on the nightstand. He lit the butt and rolled back on his pillow, staring at the yellowed ceiling. A cockroach scurried across the cheap stucco finish.

"Nice digs you brought me to, darling," Alison laughed as she took the cigarette from Rager and pulled a drag from it.

"It's the only place this side of town that rents by the hour, babe," Rager winked. "Besides, who cares where we are? I only have eyes for you."

"Oh pull-eeez!" Alison laughed. "You don't have a romantic bone in your entire body, do you, tough guy?"

"What makes you say that?" Rager asked.

"Most guys would at least light a cigarette for me after they screwed me," Alison smirked. "I had to steal yours."

Rager got up and began pulling his pants on.

"We're all done?" Alison wore a puzzled look.

"Gotta go to work," Rager offered.

"It's 11-o'clock, Kent," she exclaimed. "Graveyard shift?"

"You could say that," Rager reasoned.

"I thought you said you were your own boss?" Alison asked as she noticed small burn marks all over Rager's back and neck.

"Look," Rager said as he pulled a black t-shirt over his thin frame. "I won't ask you a lot of questions. I expect the same in return, okay?"

"Yes, sir!" Alison saluted. "Not a problem – trust me"

Rager leaned in and kissed Alison. "You are one groovy chick, baby."

Alison blushed and put her palm on Rager's cheek.

"Let's not make this a one-nighter, okay, Kent?"

"Don't worry about that, sweetheart," Rager grinned. "I'll meet you at Big Boys tomorrow night. Maybe 8 o'clock?"

"Groovy," Alison said. "See you there!"

Rager grabbed his leather coat and slipped out the door.

Alison looked around the room. She grimaced as she saw the cockroach headed down the opposite wall.

"What a shithole," she hissed. "Haven't they ever heard of Pine-Sol?"

* * * * * * *

Ralph glanced at his watch as he sat in his ratty '66 Chevelle SS. He did a double take and then rolled his eyes. He looked over at Stan, who was picking a scab off his forearm.

"Shit man, I forgot to wind this thing! Rager's gonna be royally pissed-off if we're late," Ralph whined.

Ralph pulled the watch off his wrist and beat it to death on the steering wheel.

"Wasn't worth a damn anyhow," Ralph huffed.

"You know? They say someday those watches will run for a year on one tiny battery," Stan offered. "It's space age science – that NASA stuff."

"Oh shut the hell up with that *Natural Enquirer* bullshit, Stan!" Ralph blurted. "That's the dumbest shit I ever heard!"

Abruptly, Rager's Boss 429 appeared next to Stan's window, just as Stan flicked his scab out. It bounced off Rager's coat sleeve and into the Mustang.

"What the hell was that?" Rager demanded.

Stan shrugged, "I dunno."

"It was his bloody scab, Rage!" Ralph laughed. "He picked it of his arm and told me he was gonna flip it on ya! Ha ha ha!"

Stan turned back to Rager, "No Rage, it wasn't th…."

Stan's excuse was interrupted by Rager's burning Lucky Strike, which hit him in the forehead. The burning embers sizzled on Stan's eyelashes.

"Ohh man!" Stan cried out as he rubbed his eyes. "I'm sorry, Rage!"

"Where 'we at?" Rager demanded.

"The LS6 just came in," Ralph offered. "Dude parked it under the street light and went into his girl's house. The lights went out five minutes later, so I'll bet he's poundin' it to that sweet lil' thing right now."

"Yeah! I seen her coming home earlier," Stan offered. "She looks like that Peggy Soup chick from Mod Squad!"

"Peggy Soup chick?" Ralph puzzled. "What the heck are you talking about?"

"It's Lipton... Peggy Lipton," Rager corrected. "Stan just shut your mouth till we're done here?

"Gotcha, Rage!" Stan grinned and gave Rager a thumbs-up.

"Ralph stepped out of his Chevelle as Rager exited the Mustang and got into the passenger seat. Stan took over at the wheel of the Chevelle.

"Are we set?" Rager asked.

"Good to go, Rage," Ralph said.

"Stan, flip the lights on if someone's coming in – high beams if it's the pigs," Rager instructed. "And don't get distracted picking scabs, okay?"

"I know the drill," Stan nodded.

Ralph gunned the Boss 429 down the street, then cut the engine at a safe distance. The Mustang drifted in and stopped just as Rager exited.

In less than twenty seconds, Rager was inside the 1970 Chevelle SS. He slide-hammered the column ignition out and shoved a screwdriver into the slot. Giving a nod to Ralph, they fired both engines at the exact same time. Ralph moved out quickly, with Rager tailing closely behind.

At the far end of the street, Stan observed the two cars moving off. He turned the key – the big 396 burped to life. Stan pulled a quick three-point turn and scurried out of the neighborhood.

Ferndale, Michigan, 11PM

Quentin Seymour locked the door to his ramshackle garage and climbed into the driver's seat of Lucas Fischer's Challenger R/T. He turned the ignition key over. The big 440 churned and burped while the laboring starter whirred with its familiar Chrysler whine.

"C'mon, my baby," Quentin whispered as he gave the pedal a few quick pumps.

Abruptly, the engine caught and bellowed out a nasty rumble of intense brawn. The Challenger idled roughly as Quentin exited the car  and popped the hood. He pulled a small screwdriver from his shirt pocket and adjusted the fuel mix on the carburetors.

"Man, it's a real bitch to get these carbs dancin' with each other," he lamented to himself as he turned the idle up a notch. "That oughta get 'er."

Quenting jumped back into the Challenger and burped the accelerator. The car growled again, then calmed back down to a rough – but rhythmic – idle. He pulled the pistol-grip shift knob back and eased out the clutch; the rumbling Challenger echoed down the driveway between a tall fence and a three-family slum and exited into the street. Quentin gave it a touch of gas and the car moved out effortlessly.

Rolling down the main thoroughfare, Quentin could feel the eyes of motorists and pedestrians alike as the car thundered along. Quentin applied a smidgeon more gas as he rolled up the entry ramp to Route 696. Quentin deliberately approached the freeway slowly and as he arrived near the merge, he suddenly shifted down to first, clutched and wound the engine RPMs up. As the mill roared, he popped the clutch. Quentin didn't expect the amount of torque he had just unleashed. His head banged against the headrest and he could feel the G's on his torso as he pulled hard for 2nd gear. The tires had squealed through most of second gear when Quentin shoved the pistol grip forward to 3rd. At this point, the Challenger was already 15mph over the posted speed limit, and by the time Quentin banged 4th gear, he was approaching hyper-speed and on his way to a distant galaxy.

Late at night on Route 696, the police were usually busting-up drag races on the side roads – leaving the highway relatively free of any speed traps or cruising troopers. Quentin took the Challenger up to 130mph before he backed off on the gas pedal and gave the brakes a few pumps. Back at 80mph, he cruised along with ease until he arrived at an overpass bridge near East 11-Mile. Knowing he could start there and reach a white stripe at exactly a quarter mile away, he came to a complete stop on the highway.

Stan and Ralph had painted the line across the highway on a moonless September night, and Quentin had used the marker many times to gauge how much his upgrades would benefit his customers' Mustangs, Torinos and Cougars whenever they faced a challenge.

Quentin flipped-on Luke's line-lock switch and cranked the RPMs up to 3,000. He eased out on the clutch – causing the rear end to start its own version of twerking. The tires began belching white smoke from the wheel wells of the Challenger and when Q was certain he's achieved maximum tack on the rubber, he clicked a stopwatch and released the line-lock. The Challenger lurched forward like a leopard on its prey and was gone in an instant.

Quentin gripped onto the steering wheel as he banged the next three gears with his right hand. As he crossed the stripe, he clicked-off the stopwatch and brought the 120mph monster back down to the legal speed limit of 60.

The stopwatch read, 10.9 seconds.

Quentin grinned and took the very next exit. It was time to call Rager, collect his cash and hand the purple Challenger back over to Luke.

"This fast cat's gonna make a lotta green for those white boys," Quentin laughed as he rounded the cloverleaf and headed back from where he came. As he traveled down the ramp heading west, he goosed the car again and screamed onto 696.

"Wooooo-hooo!"

CHAPTER 11

Purple Reign

Luke Fischer drummed his thumbs nervously on the table as he peered out the plate glass window at Big Boy's Burgers. He craned his neck each time a set of headlights pulled into the lot.

"Where the Hell is he?" Luke whined as he drummed on the table again.

"Don't worry, he'll be here soon," Rager said as he swigged down a glass of cola. "And quit drumming on my table or I'll break your damn thumbs off."

Luke sat back, folded his arms and huffed.

"It's a Friday night! I could be out making money right this very minute!" Luke barked.

"There are plenty of nights ahead, Junior," Rager assured him. "We missed the mark tonight, but I've got a little action scheduled for you tomorrow night."

"Really??" Luke squealed. "I'm ready! I hope my car is!"

No sooner had the word left Luke's lips than commotion erupted in the parking lot. The Challenger R/T had arrived and its exhaust note left no doubt that the car was now packing heat.

Luke jumped from his seat and ran for the exit door – in his excitement pushing aside Alison as she returned from the ladies room.

"What's with junior?" Alison asked.

"Ah, nothing really," Rager shook his head as he poked at his fries with a fork. "I just got the kid hooked-up with my mechanic."

"You boys and your toys," Alison sighed.

"Now we're talking!" Luke yelled out as he ran across the lot toward his Challenger and Quentin.

Quentin had just locked the car and turned to see Luke charging at him like a mad bull. He tossed the keys into the air and stepped aside – watching Luke snag them like a leaping outfielder.

"Rage inside?" Quentin asked as Luke unlocked the Mopar.
"Yeah, he's in there!" Luke yelled back. "Thanks, Q!"

Luke slammed the car door shut before Quentin could mutter, "you're welcome."

With a turn of the ignition key, the big 440 blurted out an ominous exhaust note that drowned out to background sounds of the busy Woodward Avenue.

Lucas Fischer was back in his realm again after what he considered to be the longest day of his entire life. He squealed with delight as he tapped the accelerator and bounded the car forward.

He maneuvered down the exit drive to the edge of Woodward Avenue and disappeared faster (and louder) than a missile launch.

Quentin scanned the crowd inside Big Boy's until he spotted Rager and his new blond squeeze, Alison.

Rager motioned for Quentin to sit, but Quentin shook off the invite – patiently waiting for Rager to finish chewing his burger.

"Any additional damage?" Rager asked as he wiped his mouth.

"Yeah, man," Quentin said nervously, not wanting to anger Rager. "I had to go with Hooker Headers and get some pipe bent. I also popped an Isky in it. If you want this kid to win, you needed a lil' more cam. Know what I mean?"

"What's the hit then?" Rager asked.

"With labor, it'll be another $200," Quentin shrugged. "Sorry, man."

Rager looked Quentin in the eye.

"You're getting a little expensive lately, Q," Rager sneered, before popping a grin. "We want the kid to win and if that takes more green then I'm okay payin' it."

Quentin breathed a sigh of relief.

Rager whipped out a bankroll and slid two hundred dollar bills over to Quentin. "That's a thousand bucks worth of 100% pure beef we've got in that grape-colored wagon. Let's see if she can run with the big boys."

"Thanks, Rage," Quentin said as he scooped the cash and exited.

Alison smirked at Rager. "What exactly do you do for work? I mean, with all that cash stuffed into your pockets, Kent?" she asked.

"I'm into investments," Rager shrugged. "Lots and lots of investments. Some are legal. Others? Not so much."

"Drugs?" Alison asked.

"No," he answered coldly. "I stay away from that shit. I don't need the aggravation dealing with social mutants, junkies, slacker potheads and the law."

"Good," nodded Alison. "I've been there. Freaks are always a bummer."

"That's the last time we talk about what I do, okay?" Rager glared.

"Hey, no hassles, babe," Alison replied.

From the far side of Big Boy's, Denny sat – utterly detached from the Mopar gang's bench racing discussion – and sadly observed as Alison smiled and tended to Rager.

* * * * * * * *

Still burning from their heated tryst on the overlook, Tucker and Dawn cruised into Big Boy's parking lot with the top down, despite the low-50s outside temperature.

"Just checkin' in," Tucker told Dawn as he swung her Galaxie into a parking spot.

Their timing couldn't have been any worse; Rager, Alison, Stan and Ralph had exited Big Boy's and were crossing the lot toward their cars. Rager did a double take then decided it was time to drop a hand grenade.

"Well, well, well," he laughed through an exhale of cigarette smoke. "Look at the two mush-headed lovebirds. It looks like you two just got down n' dirty up at the point. Am I right?"

Tucker glared at Rager. "We have the top down, numb nuts."

"Oh, right, right," Rager gushed. "The old "top-down excuse." I get it, man. I get it."

"Screw you, Kent!" Dawn barked. "Mind your own business, you bastard!"

"Looks like I just pushed all the right buttons, huh babe?" Rager winked. "Hey, baby-killer, make sure you don some skin, man. That chick's seen some action."

On that note, Tucker exited the car as Rager walked away. He grabbed Kent by the back of his leather jacket and spun him around.

"You and me got some unfinished business, Rager!" Tucker sneered. "But you keep your nasty comments to yourself until the day comes when I knock you back down like I did before."

Abruptly, Stan and Ralph appeared – each wielding large pipe wrenches. Their heads were cocked as they both puffed on cigarettes.

"You didn't knock me anywhere, scrote," Rager bit back. "You just got lucky and I had a bad day – a *very rare* bad day. But I'm back... and you'd better watch your back, chump."

Tucker released Rager's lapels as Stan and Ralph took a step closer.

"You'll never win, Rager," Tucker retorted. "You'll always be number two around here. And we all know what happens to number two."

Stan looked around at everyone, "Ha ha! It gets flushed! Right?"

As customary, Rager fired his cigarette at Stan's face – hitting him in the throat. "I told you to shut your face when I'm talking to someone!"

Stan took a step backward – wiping ash from his Adam's apple.

Oblivious to it all, Alison giggled, "Who's that girl? Is that your ex, Kent? I know her. She's very nice"

"Just get in the car, Alison," Rager said calmly.

Tucker stormed back to Dawn's car. "I've seen enough here. Let's go catch a movie or something."

Tucker fired-up the Galaxie and dashed out of the parking lot.

* * * * * *

In making his quick escape, Tucker missed his opportunity to see a major confrontation – for only seconds later, Luke's purple Challenger returned to the parking lot at Big Boy's. In tow, were several other vehicles and at the end…. a 1970 Chevelle SS LS6 dressed in black with white striping. Luke exited his Mopar and made a beeline for Rager.

"Mr. Rager! Mr. Rager!" he cried out breathlessly. "I'm glad you're still here! This guy in the Chevy… the black one? He wants to go!".

Rager took a long gaze at the Chevelle "You sure you wanna break-in your grape jelly bean against that beast?"

"Yes, yes! I do!" Luke nodded. "I'm ready!"

Rager lit a cigarette and hunkered toward the Chevelle with Luke following along behind him.

"When I talk," Rager warned him, "you shut your fat little pie hole. Got it?"

"Got it, Mr. Rager!" Luke replied.

"And call me Rager," Kent added. "I don't like that "mister" crap."

Rager approached the Chevelle as the driver stepped out. He was big and husky with a scraggly beard. Rager shook his hand and the negotiation began. From afar, the discussion became quite animated.

"What's he doing?" Alison asked Ralph.

"He's pimpin' the kid, sweetie pie," Ralph replied.

"What do you mean?" Alison asked.

"Rage is his manager. The kid wants to race the Chevy, but Rage is bank."

"So he gets a cut off the top?" Alison asked.

"Ha, are you kidding?" Ralph quipped. "He takes it all and throws the kid a bone."

"That explains a lot," Alison whispered to herself.

Rager walked quickly back to the gang, then turned to a growing throng of spectators. "Let's go, people!" he yelled. '14 Mile Road east to Crooks, then head north toward Troy. There's a marked half-mile strip this guy's gonna lead us to. He says the pigs don't even know about it."

The crowd made haste to their cars. Doors slammed and engines rumbled to life as they all vied to be first out of the parking lot.
Rager turned to Lucas and his comrades. "That Chevy is a bone-stock LS6. But that's *still* 454 cubic inches of bowtie bad news with 450 ponies under the hood."

"What's the action?" Stan asked.

"Five bills," Rager answered. "Rolling start and no drafting."

"Groovy! No problem at all," Luke grinned.

"We'll see about that," Rager returned.

* * * * * * *

Bubba Baker rolled his black Chevelle SS to a stop on the long stretch of dark country lane just off Crooks Road. The big driver stepped out of his car and motioned the following drivers to spread out along the shoulders.

A single light post illuminated a powder blue paint stripe that was roughly painted across the paved road. Bubba pulled up to the line and shut down his engine.

Moments later, the amazing, combined rumble of Rager's Boss 429 and Luke's 440 6-pack drew all attention to their arrival. Luke pulled the Challenger along side of the Chevelle, while Rager parked his Mustang and helped Alison exit the car. Nearby, Stan and Ralph parked the '66 Chevelle and grabbed a flashlight and a milk crate from the trunk for Rager to stand on.

Rager waved off the milk crate, while gathering Lucas and his thugs together in a makeshift huddle.

"Listen up, girls," Rager said in a low whisper. "I ain't making the pre-race speech. We're not going to intimidate this Chevelle dude at all. He's a big, strong farm boy and ex-Marine. I don't want my spine broken again and I'm sure you guys don't want to tangle with him either."

"That ain't like you, Rage," Ralph lamented. "We never back down from no one."

Rager raised a finger and stuck it firmly into Ralph's forehead. "When I say, *don't poke the bees nest*, I mean, *don't* poke the damn bees nest. Got it?"

"Yeah, we got it, Rage," Stan answered.

"Okay. Let's win this and get the hell outa here," Rager ordered.

The $500 in cash was collected from each driver and they entered their vehicles. For the first time ever, Lucas felt nervous; he'd never been involved in such a formal drag racing match-up and he'd never had someone stake $500 on his driving ability.

Rager sensed his nervousness as Luke grinned and gave Rager a thumbs-up. He stopped and leaned into Luke's car.

"This guy's got a fast car and you have a fast car. Big difference? He's got 250-lbs of weight on him. You're a skinny little shit and that's your advantage. Shift well and you'll win without a problem."

"Gotcha, Rager," Luke nodded.

Rager walked several paces out beyond the two cars.

"Gentlemen, burn 'em!" he yelled.

At once, both cars broke into a combined, massive display of white tire smoke. The tires screamed a torturous, high-pitched squeal, as the combined 1,000 horsepower of both cars broke loose and rolled forward.

Rager directed them to reverse back. Properly tacked, the duel was ready to begin.

Rager waited until both cars were 50-yards back from the blue start line. He raised a flashlight and illuminated it. The two cars lurched forward, albeit slowly and reached a speed of 25 miles per hour as they approached the line.

Abruptly, a war broke out.

The Chevelle SS seemed to leap from the pavement as full pedal was applied to the accelerator, while Luke's Challenger just plowed forward – fully grounded.

Both cars were head-to-head as they screamed down the country road toward the next illuminated streetlight. Strangely, all the other lights between the two points were non-functional.

Lucas focused on the road ahead while keeping the blurred image of the Chevelle within his peripheral vision. He leaned in slightly and pulled back hard into 2nd gear – a perfect shift! The rear wheels chirped as the tires broke free of asphalt due to the massive torque. Suddenly, the black Chevelle was no longer in the corner of Luke's eye. The Chevelle was not being beaten, however; Bubba was merely ringing-out first-gear. As he bang-shifted 2nd, the Chevelle vaulted forward and slightly ahead of Lucas' Challenger.

"Oh, shit!" Lucas yelled as he saw the lunging SS break by.

Both drivers held onto 2nd gear until almost red line before slamming their shift knobs forward into 3rd gear and –again– both cars left a short strip of burnt rubber upon the blacktop.

At this point, Rager's assessment rang true: the lighter Challenger and featherweight driver was becoming a huge advantage to Luke as he inched past the growling Chevelle SS. As the tach approached red line, Luke braced himself, then pulled back fast, with a lightning quick pump of his clutch pedal. The Challenger sailed forward and beyond the Chevelle's straining LS6.

"Wooooo-hoo!" Luke screamed as the line loomed a football field length ahead, but the Chevelle wasn't just going to roll over.

Through his peripheral vision, Luke saw the front bumper of the Chevelle in his passenger window. Slowly, but surely, the front fender was starting to fill the view through the right side glass.

"No, no, no!" Luke cried out. "Hang-in there, baby!"

Luke pressed hard on the throttle pedal, fully believing that he could squeeze just a few drops of high-octane Esso gas through the line to his three whining carbs.

The Chevelle suddenly stopped gaining – abruptly fading back and away.

"Yes!" Luke pumped the air as he crossed the painted line in the road.

In his rearview mirror, he could see white smoke billowing from the exhaust and reverse air-induction hood scoop. He stopped and swung the Challenger back to see if the driver needed help. Luke swallowed his glee – as not to completely piss-off the ex-Marine – and rolled to a stop next to the Chevelle. Bubba stepped out of his car while Luke ran to his assistance.

"You okay, man?" Luke asked.

"Ah, yeah," he scowled. "I'm fine. Just a damn dumbass is all!"

"What the hell happened?" Luke puzzled.

"Break in time," the driver shook his head. "This engine's got 250 miles on it. That's all. I didn't give her the proper break-in time and now I done smoked a head gasket for sure!"

Luke shook his head. "Man, I hope it's only a head gasket."

Rager and crew arrived just as the driver popped the Chevelle's hood – causing a white cloud to billow up from the engine.

"Looks like some engine trouble, my friend," Rager grinned.

The big Marine wasn't in the mood for a happy exchange.

"Look," he snapped, "take your money and take little junior here and get the hell outta my face before I break someone's damn neck."

"Hey, no worries, big guy," Rager replied. "C'mon, kid, meet us back at Big Boys."

"I will!" Luke smiled before turning a more serious look toward the Chevelle driver. "Sorry about your car, man."

"Yeah, yeah… Goodbye," Bubba snapped. "Drive down to the start line and tell that cat in the tow truck to come up here, will ya?"

"No problem," Luke gave Bubba a thumbs-up as he turned away to peer inside his Chevy's engine compartment.

CHAPTER 12

Bankrupt Streets – Bankrupt Values

Over the weeks that followed, Rager arranged five or six street duels per week for Lucas Fischer and his Plum Crazy Purple Challenger R/T. The money was as good as the winning was consistent – as were the barbs and abrasive verbal assaults from Luke. Knowing that he had Kent Rager and his two thugs, Stan and Ralph covering his back he'd become more obnoxious than ever –.

Soon, every street racer from Waterford down to Dearborn was gunning for Luke and his Dodge, while others just wanted to knock him on his ass.

Rager was passing-off a hot n' loaded 1970 Buick Riviera at Dick Sturgis' chop shop when Dick passed the word to him that The Ramchargers wanted Luke Fischer out of the district.

"The Ramchargers want him to disappear – says the kid's givin' Mopars a bad vibe," Dick warned Rager. "They said to kick him back to Grosse Point. Maybe race him up in Clinton or New Haven, but get him the hell outta the Royal Oak area of Woodward, they told me."

Rager wasn't going to relent. He knew the pressure was on the others to beat Luke's Challenger, so there was plenty of money still to be made.

"Screw the Ramchargers," Rager scoffed. "They're just a bunch of factory nerds with too much money in their pockets. We'll beat them too."

As far as Rager was concerned, he'd be pimping Luke's Challenger on or around Woodward Avenue until nobody dared or

122

cared to race him any longer, but there seemed to be no shortage of willing competitors.

What Rager didn't know was that Sgt. Harlan Boggs of the Royal Oak Police Department was also gunning for Luke Fischer. You couldn't run up and down Woodward in a bright purple, low-squatting, thunder-spitting Challenger R/T – night after night – without drawing the attention of local law enforcement.

Until now, Rager had kept a step ahead of Boggs by demanding that the street racing take place in remote areas to the north or west of the Loop, but it wasn't hard for Boggs to gather information from other drivers when they could avoid a speeding ticket by answering some of his questions about the purple Dodge. Little-by-little, Boggs had compiled a pretty good file on Rager's favorite back road racing strips. All he needed now was to catch Luke in the act and nail Rager on a *contributing to the delinquency of a minor* charge.

* * * * * * *

Tucker exited the repair shop office and turned to lock the door for the night. In the door glass, he could see the reflection of a bright red car behind him in the garage. He turned to see Hoyt – wrenching under the hood of Tucker's '65 GTO.

"When did this come in? Tucker asked.

Hoyt pulled his head out from under the hood, wearing a mischievous grin as he wiped a spark plug clean.

"I swung by the barn at lunch today," Hoyt winked. "Seems like somebody needs a dose of street action to get himself on the right track again."

"So, I'm going racing tonight?" Tucker asked.

"No. *We* are going racing tonight," Hoyt laughed. "I already told Dawn to meet us later for a late night snack at Big Boy's. She's the one who suggested that you need to let off some steam – said you're wound-up tighter than an Accel Coil."

Hoyt laughed as Tucker shook his head.

123

"Looks like I'm going racing tonight, buddy," Tucker said.

"I've checked and lubed all the linkage on your trips," Hoyt advised. "Ran a compression check on the 428. Looks good. I even gassed it up on the way with some Sunoco 104. We'll be a force to reckon with!"

"I reckon we'll wreck 'em," Tucker joked.

Tucker tossed his old leather briefcase into the backseat of the GTO while Hoyt closed the hood and fastened the hood pins.

"I can already feel the adrenaline rush!" he yelled as he ran to the washbasin to clean up.

"Cool your jets, Hoyt," Tucker yelled after him. "I've still gotta go home and shower and shave."

Tucker turned the dash key and the tri-powered tiger burped to life. He gave it a few revs before pulling it even with the garage door. He blasted the horn.

Hoyt came running out from the washroom, "Alright! Alright!" he yelled.

Hoyt pulled hard on the chain pulley, opening the garage door just high enough for Tucker to slide the Pontiac through. Hoyt let the steel door slam down, exited through the shop door and leaped through the GTO's passenger window.

Tucker burped the throttle a few more times, then dumped the clutch and lurched the car out with two long strips of rubber.

The car disappeared in a dense fog of smoke and high-octane exhaust.

* * * * * * * * *

Things were just getting underway at Big Boy's as Denny Stark swung in with his '69 Roadrunner. As always, he scanned the parking lot, hoping to spot Alison's powder-blue Pinto. Denny would also look for the black Boss 429. If he had any hope of talking to Alison again, he'd have to ensure that Kent Rager was nowhere to be found.

As luck would have it, tonight was a rare night where Alison's Pinto was parked under the trees and there was no sign of Rager's Mustang.

Denny carefully parked a few cars away from Alison's car. He set his parking brake – having learned that Stan and Ralph could roll his car away at any time – and double-checked his door locks before heading inside the burger joint.

Denny had no idea how he'd approach Alison, but he knew that he'd find something... anything... to talk about.

* * * * * * *

Edie Knox looked up from her kitchen sink as a red GTO lumbered up the gravel road to the Knox family's farmhouse.

"Alvin! Tucker's home!" she yelled into the adjoining parlor, where Tucker's father chain-smoked while reading the daily newspaper.

Edie removed her apron and walked through the front screen door to greet Tucker and Hoyt.

As the boys approached the front porch steps, Edie removed a ribbon she'd used to hold her hair back while preparing dinner. Her long blond locks spilled over her slim shoulders. At 48-years old, Edie had preserved the stunning beauty that earned her the *1941 Montrose High School Homecoming Queen* title. Well-tanned and lean from her love of gardening, she contrasted nicely against her light yellow sundress.

Everyone in the greater Royal Oak area who knew him was convinced that Will Hoyt was so deep into the motorhead culture that he simply had no time for females, but the sad truth was that Hoyt was immersed in a decade-long crush on Tucker's mother, Edie Knox.

As Edie stood on the porch, waiting for the boys to trudge up the stairs, Hoyt stopped and looked up. He let out an audible sigh as he saw the light spring breeze blowing through Edie's hair.

Tucker turned back toward him. "Are you okay, buddy?" he asked.

"Oh, uh... yeah," Hoyt stammered. "I'm just tired. You know, long day?"

"Yeah, I hear you, man," Tucker nodded.

Edie greeted each boy with a hug. She became somewhat perplexed when Hoyt held onto his hug a little longer.

"Umm... yeah, okay. Why don't you guys have a seat on the porch and I'll bring you some nice cold lemonade?" Edie suggested. "I've got spaghetti and meatballs on the stove. Homemade!"

"I've gotta shower first, Mom," Tucker resisted. "And I think we're eating at Big B..."

Tucker was interrupted by Hoyt's enthusiasm. "We'd *love* to have spaghetti, Mrs. Knox!"

"Wonderful, William!" Edie beamed as Tucker rolled his eyes and headed inside. "Let me get you a glass of lemonade then. You're probably thirsty after working so hard all day."

"Yes...yes I am, Mrs. Knox," Hoyt replied.

"Oh gosh, William," Edie laughed, "Please call me Edie from now on. You and Tucker are grown men now. Very handsome grown men, I might add!"

Hoyt felt his heart thumping in his chest as he flashed a foolish grin at Edie. "That's sounds great, Mrs. Kn.... I mean, Edie." He gulped.

Edie paused for a moment to take-in Hoyt's peculiar reaction before turning to go back inside the house. Hoyt couldn't see the all-knowing smirk on Edie's face as she walked away.

* * * * * * * *

Denny entered the noisy scene at Big Boys to the blaring jukebox sound of the *Five Stairsteps*.

> *Ooo-oo-Child, things are gonna get easier…*
> *Ooo-oo-child, things'll get brighter….*

"Aw, man! Are you *kiddin'* me?" Denny scoffed loudly.

Denny spotted Alison as quickly as she'd spotted Denny. She smiled and gave a little half-wave, which was enough for Denny to read as an invitation. He made his way through the crowd to her booth.

"Hi Alison," he grinned nervously. "Mind if I sit down?"

"Hi, 383!" Alison laughed. "Please do!"

Denny slid-in to the bench seat opposite from Alison.

"I was just kidding," Alison laughed. "You're Denny, right?"

Denny's eyes lit-up – Alison had remembered his name after all. "Yes, I'm still Denny," he joked. "How's that baby-blue Pinto treating you?"

"Oh it's wonderful. So much torque!" Alison joked. "Ford has a better idea. You know?"

"Yes, I've heard that rumor," Denny laughed then his demeanor shifted. "Won't you be in big, big trouble if Rager sees me sitting here with you?"

"Of course not," Alison laughed, "but *you* will!"

"Oh. Ha, yeah... I get it," Denny chuckled. "I'll take my chances."

"Denny?" Alison asked, as she looked deep into his eyes, "Why is everyone so afraid of Kent Rager? I mean, like, what does he do when he's out late at night?"

Denny furtively scanned the diner before leaning in toward Alison. "You really wanna know?" he asked.

"Yes, I do," she nodded.

"It's not just street racing," Denny whispered. "He jacks cars. Kent and his two thugs, they are some bad cats."

"They steal cars..." Alison quavered. "Oh my God. How did I not see it?"

Denny looked around him again. If anyone saw him whispering to Alison and told Rager, his beloved Roadrunner would look like the coyote had finally caught up to it.

"Alison, you know I'm attracted to you," Denny stammered, "but even if you have zero interest in me, that's okay, but you've got to get away from Rager. He's dangerous. At the least, you could end up in jail for being an accessory to grand theft."

"No shit! Really?" Alison cried out, causing others nearby to peer over at her.

Denny spotted Rager's Boss Mustang pulling into the Big Boy's parking lot.

"Kent's here," Denny whispered. "I'd better move."

"Denny?" Alison looked up at Denny. "I *do* like you. You're a pretty groovy guy. I guess I just need to find a way out of this."

Denny reached down and squeezed Alison's hand.

"Be safe. I'll do whatever I can to help you," Denny offered.

* * * * * * *

At the small card table on the Knox family's long porch, Hoyt was enthusiastically finishing his final few bites of Edie's spaghetti and homemade meatballs as she sat across from him – amused by his voracious appetite.

Behind her, Tucker and Alvin talked shop over their own bowls of Italian cuisine. Alvin sipped on a glass of burgundy.

"This is the best tasting meal I've ever had, Mrs… I mean, Edie!" Hoyt blurted through a mouthful of pasta. "I hope you'll call me every time you make this again!"

"Why thank you, William!" Edie beamed before leaning back and crossing her legs.

Hoyt's eyes were immediately drawn to her velvety, tanned legs as her sundress rode up her thigh, causing him to choke on a meatball.

"Now William, chew your food properly," she joked. "There's *plenty* more inside!"

"I'm okay, Edie," Hoyt said as he waived her off. "This is just so good. I mean, they are very, very good."

Edie saw Hoyt glance at her legs and sensed a hint of double entendre in his words, but rather than brushing them off, she fed into it.

"Yes, William," she smiled, "They are… very, very good… and so tender."

In shock that Edie was volleying right back at him, Hoyt choked again. He looked up at Edie, who was coquettishly grinning at him.

* * * * * * *

Tucker swung onto Woodward Avenue and gave the GTO some gas. The car responded quickly and smoothly – a testament to Hoyt's expertise. He decided to press the pedal to the floor, allowing the other two carbs to kick-in. The big 428 growled, then responded with neck-snapping acceleration.

"Man, I love the sound of those Trips sucking wind," Hoyt laughed as they tore along the avenue. "And the way this baby gets up and goes is incredible!"

"There's only one feeling that's better!" Tucker chuckled.

"Don't even go there, man," Hoyt frowned.

Tucker could only smile as he downshifted, then goosed the throttle for a quick chirp of the rear tires and some additional growl from the dual pipes.

"You seemed pretty enthusiast about my mom's meatballs," Tucker smirked.

"Well, they were delicious," Hoyt bounced back. "You're mom's such an amazing lady too."

Tucker shot Hoyt a steely look.

"What do you mean, Willie?"

"Nothing, man," Hoyt replied with a nervous quiver. "She's just the perfect wife and mother and cook and she's pretty and…"

"Yeah, that's enough, Hoyt," Tucker snapped.

"I'm just sayin…" Hoyt frowned.

"Well stop sayin' then," Tucker replied. "and whatever you're thinking, stop thinking it."

Hoyt sighed and leaned back in his seat. In his mind, he was convinced that he'd just crossed a thin line with Tucker. He would have to tone things down a few notches around Edie, or else he'd put his friendship with Tucker in jeopardy.

"My mom is pretty cool though," Tucker added with a grin plastered across his face.

"Yeah, brother, she is," Hoyt sighed.

Tucker slowed the GTO and stopped for a red light just as a bright yellow '69 Camaro SS arrived next to them. The driver burped the gas pedal and waited.

Tucker looked over at the driver, who was staring straight ahead.

"This cat wants to go," Hoyt whispered.

"I know," chuckled Tucker, "I'm just making him work for it."

The driver of the Camaro SS roared a much longer rev, then turned to look at Hoyt. He flashed two twenty-dollar bills.

"Wanna run for forty bills?" Hoyt asked Tucker.

"Sure," Tucker said. "Give him a nod."

Hoyt looked over and winked at the Camaro SS driver as Tucker applied a long responding rev from the bowels of the GTO. Hoyt opened the door and stood on the sill, scanning the area for cruisers.

"We're clear!" he yelled loud enough for the SS driver to hear.

Hoyt swung back inside the GTO just as the light went green.

Both cars slowly passed through the intersection, spewing clouds of white smoke from their wheel wells, but once the rubber grabbed, the cars were catapulted forward – simultaneously banging 2nd gear.

The cars stayed even all the way through 2nd, but when 3rd, gear was activated via a perfect power shift, the GTO leaped ahead of the Camaro by a car length. But the SS was only hitting its stride as the cars shifted into 4th gear. They evened out again as the next light approached. Luckily, the light had just turned green, meaning both cars could power through the intersection before slowing to settle up.

"You're okay, Tuck!" Hoyt screamed. "Just keep it on the floor!"

Slowly, but surely, the GTO inched ahead of the SS until they had a fender on it as they crossed the intersection.

"Woooo-hoo!" Hoyt yelled as Tucker downshifted and slowed the car, pulling into a strip mall parking area. The Camaro pulled up along side and handed his cash over to Hoyt.

"Pretty fast car for a 389," the driver offered. "I thought my big ol' 396 would whoop its ass, but I figured wrong, I reckon!"

"You're not from around here, are you?" Hoyt observed as the driver spat a chunk of chaw onto the pavement.

"Naw, I'm from Georgia," the driver grinned. "Jus' up here visitin' my sister and her husband. They had a lil' rug rat and I reckoned I'd come up and meet 'er."

"Why are you out racing" Tucker asked.

"Oh man, I just 'bout run outa cash," he laughed. "Gotta make some gas and toll cash to get me back home!"

Tucker nudged Hoyt.

"No!" whispered Hoyt.

"C'mon, Hoyt, I'll buy dinner tonight."

"Yeah? Well okay then," Hoyt huffed as he handed the cash back to the Camaro SS driver. "Here, take this back, man. Come on over to

Big Boys and I'll point out a few dogs that you're guaranteed to beat."

"That sounds like a good deal," the driver grinned. "Thank ya!"

Both cars rolled out of the lot, headed for Big Boy's Burgers.

"You've gotta love a guy like that," Hoyt exclaimed. "He came all the way from Georgia to visit family and now he's living it on the streets – racing for gas money."

"We'll get him to race Denny, Tucker laughed. "That SS will eat that Roadrunner for a quick 50."

"We'd do well to warn him about Luke Fisher and Rager too," Hoyt nodded.

"I know of a Duster 340 he could hand an ass-whoopin' to," Tucker laughed.

"Real funny, Tuck," Hoyt shot back. "You should be on Laugh-In!"

Tucker applied some gas to the pedal and the Goat burbled off toward Big Boy's.

CHAPTER 13

Alison Chambers: Private Shoe

Kent Rager reached for his pack of Lucky Strikes in the dim light of the motel room. He pulled out two cigarettes and lit them simultaneously – handing one to Alison.

Alison couldn't help but notice the burn marks on Rager's upper arms and shoulders – a testament to his rough upbringing – but Alison assumed they were scars left by his accident when he'd flipped his last '70 Mustang after his loss to Tucker a year before. Little did she know that Rager's alcoholic father used lit cigarettes as his favorite form of discipline when Kent was just a boy.

"I appreciate that you found us a nicer motel," Alison quipped. "The last time we did this I was cornered by cockroaches after you left."

Rager chuckled out a breath of smoke. "It's amazing what an extra ten bucks will get you."

"So are you going to desert me here again, like the last time?" she asked.

"No way, babe," Rager assured her. "I've got this pad for the night. I do have to leave, but I'll be back before 3AM. I'll wake you up and we can do a little repeat. Then I'll take you to breakfast."

Alison took a drag off her cigarette, fighting back the impulse to ask where Rager was going, but she lost the battle with her conscience.

"Where exactly are you going this late at night?" she asked.

"I told you already not to ask what I do, didn't I?" Rager spat as he sat up on the edge of the bed.

Rager turned and gave her a steely look that seemed to pierce her soul. Alison could feel an adrenaline rush pulsing through her. Fear. Her survival instinct had kicked-in and she had never felt so threatened.

Despite the fact that her heart was pumping double-time, she reasoned that it was now or never.

"I want to know, Kent," Alison said as she garnered more courage to face off with him. "We're together a lot lately and I don't know who you are, or what you do. I don't want to find myself in some kind of shit storm that I can't find my way out of."

Rager didn't answer. He turned away and pulled his white tank t-shirt over his head, then reached for his cigarette.

"I heard a rumor you steal cars," Alison blurted – spontaneously deciding it was time to get everything out in the open. "Is that true?"

"Now who the hell told you that?" Rager spit.

"That doesn't matter," Alison hissed. "I want to know if it's true and if it's not true, I want to know what you do when you leave me in a cheap motel at eleven o'clock every time we hook up."

Rager paused, then exhaled a long breath of cigarette smoke from his lungs. "Okay, look," he said turning back toward her, "I don't steal cars. I work for a guy in a chop shop as a receiver. He pays me to hang there all night and check out the boosts that come in. If the car is what he wants, I pay the guy who jacked it and get the crew to tear it down. If the car is a piece of shit, I reject it and send the guy to a junkyard where he can get a little scratch for it. That's it. That's all I do."

"So you deal in stolen cars and pay kids to street race for you," Alison replied with some measured sarcasm. "Great."

"Look," Rager paused as he again stared deeply into Alison's eyes. "I was in a bad car wreck a year and a half ago. When I got out of the hospital, my old job was gone. This was the only thing I could do since the union was on strike."

"You're UAW?" Alison asked.

"Aren't we all?" Rager answered. "I was an quality control guy at Dearborn. I checked out the Mustangs and Cougars."

"You worked at The Rouge?" Alison was a bit taken aback. "My old man works at Rouge Complex. He's some kind of pencil pusher."

"Yeah…. The Rouge plant," Rager lied as he stood up to tuck in his shirt.

"Are you going back when the strike ends?" Alison asked.

Rager shrugged. "There's more to life than working on an assembly line until you have a heart attack, or a stroke, like my old man did," Rager said. "Now he just sits in front of the tube all day, smoking and drinking himself into a coma every night."

"Not cool," Alison grimaced.

"I want to open a dealership someday.," Rager grinned.

"Well, that's an admirable goal," Alison nodded. "You seem hell bent on doing it. You're driven. And quite handsome too, I might add."

Alison hoped that her compliments would calm the evil presence that seemed to have filled the entire room.
Rager bent over the bed and kissed Alison. "I'll see you in a few hours, baby. Lock the door behind me."
Rager exited as Alison rose from the bed to secure the door. She sat on the edge of the bed and took a drag off her Lucky Strike as she eyed the phone on the nightstand. She picked up the receiver, but then slammed the phone back down.

Wringing her hands, Alison walked to the window and watched Rager's Boss Mustang exit the parking lot. She picked the phone back up again and dialed a number.

"Hello, Daddy. It's me," she said. "Yes, I know it's late. I'm sorry. No, I'm fine, honest."

Alison hesitated – running her hand through her hair.

"Daddy, I need your help," she pleaded – her hands trembling. "I need you to look up the payroll records of an employee who worked at the Rouge until last year. Yes, I'm seeing him...his name is Rager....Kent Rager from Montrose. Will you do it? I just need to know if this guy is lying to me."

Alison took a final drag from her cigarette before snuffing it out on the top of her empty can of Tab.

"Thank you, Daddy," she said. "I'll come by tomorrow night around dinner time. Yes, Daddy, I'm fine! I'll see you tomorrow, okay? Bye."

Alison pulled up her jeans and slipped her Foghat concert t-shirt over her head. Pulling on her boots, she stood, grabbed her purse and exited.

* * * * * * * * *

Hoyt was screaming with delight as Tucker slammed 4th gear, sending the GTO into hyperspace. Behind Tucker's GTO, a frustrated local in a '68 Gran Sport, Mark Muenzner, was cursing at his jammed Hurst shifter, while his spasmodic left clutching foot was completely left out of the conversation.

"Amazing Mark," as he called himself at Detroit Dragway, had ground his old Hurst linkage into a loose cluster of worn out washers and stripped bolts due to his inability to coordinate shifts, but *Mr. Amazing* never blamed himself. Every week, he'd return to the drag strip at Brownstown Charter and lose his quarter-mile runs due to his ineptitude. When it came to speed shifting, Muenzner was as smooth as a mouthful of Metamucil.

Tucker turned the GTO into a closed mom and pop pharmacy and waited for Mark to catch up to him with his $50 winnings.

"I know that GS," boasted Hoyt. "He's got an Isky cam, Edelbrock intake with a Holley double-pumper and Hedmans installed on that Buick 400, but he can't drive worth a shit."

"Good car, bad driver, huh?" joked Tucker.

"Yeah, sorta like Rager," Hoyt laughed. "But Rager's a different kind of bad."

Hoyt fiddled with the GTO's AM radio until he tuned-in a rock station which was blaring sound *Edison Lighthouse*.

"Hear the guitar riff in the background of *Love Grows Where My Rosemary Goes*?" he asked. "It's actually pretty tight. These guys will be a top rock band in just a few years – just you watch!"

"I dunno," Tucker sighed as he rubbed his jaw.

Mark Muenzner arrived in his beaten Buick GS and slid up next to Tucker. He handed his fifty bucks over and shut his rumbling 400 cubic-inch mill off.

"What's the word on the streets?" Muenzner asked.

"Stay away from the little shithead in the purple Challenger is all I've heard," Tucker laughed.

"Oh yeah man," Muenzner quipped, "that dude is bad news – runs for Kent Rager now… or so I've heard."

"Hoyt's worked on that car," Tucker offered, "but someone else got their dirty mitts on it, because it sounds a lot different now."

"Probably Rager's mechanic," Muenzner offered. "Quentin Seymour. That cat knows his Fords, but he can tune just about anything to run with the big boys."

Hoyt sighed and twisted in his seat.

"Yeah, well we beat his Boss 429 last year with this Goat!" Hoyt protested. "I can build anything to outrun whatever Quentin pops out of his grubby little mouse hole."

"Sounds like you got some issues, brother," Muenzner laughed. "The bad part is that kid's gonna get all wrapped-up in Rager's car jacking business and he'll end up in jail with a gigantic fear of using the prison showers."

"Rager's got no future here," Tucker asserted. "I'd be surprised if he's not dead or in the big house before the year's out."

"By the way," Muenzner asked. "Do you guys know anything about a Camaro SS? Some southern dude drives it. He beat me out of a C-note last night on a light-to-light up on 16 Mile."

"Yeah, he's new around here – a Vietnam vet from Georgia," Tucker answered as Hoyt stifled his hysterical laughter. "He's okay – just trying to race for enough cash to get back south, I heard."

"Well, he's got my hard-earned pay," Muenzner asserted. "It was almost as if he came into Big Boy's looking for me. Kinda strange, man."

Hoyt buried his face in his hands as he tried to hold in his guffaws. This did not go unnoticed by Mark Muenzner.

"What's with Hoyt?" he asked.

"Oh, just allergies. You know spring time pollen?" Tucker offered.

"Too bad. Hey, Hoyt! I hope you feel better, man!" Muenzner called out as he sparked his GS to life. "See you guys on the boulevard!"

With a loud grinding of first gear, Muenzer eased up on his clutch and jerked the Buick off the lot.

"That poor bastard needs a Turbo-350 tranny," Hoyt chuckled. "He hasn't got a clue about 4-speeds."

"Kind of like you and music," Tucker grinned.

"And what's that supposed to mean?" Hoyt protested.

* * * * * * *

Kent Rager lit another butt as he tossed the empty cigarette package out of the Mustang. Next to him, Lucas Fischer sat, doe-eyed in disbelief that he was actually involved in something illegal.

"I don't think I should be here," Luke protested as he watched Stan and Ralph breaking into a '69 Plymouth GTX. "This seems wrong to me."

"Relax, kid," Rager commanded. "You're part of the team now. This is what we do to keep your purple pony running hard!"

Ralph pulled the door open and Stan dove into the GTX to begin hot-wiring the ignition wires.

"We'll be outa here in two minutes, kid," Rager assured Luke.

Abruptly, a large man appeared out of the shadows with a spade shovel and slammed it against the back of Ralph's head. Blood splattered across the car's windshield as Ralph fell like a sack of potatoes onto the street. The man then jammed the point of the shovel into Stan's protruding ankles.

"Aaaaaargh!" Stan's scream echoed out from inside the car and across the neighborhood as he attempted to get himself out from under the Plymouth's dashboard.

Again, the man swung his shovel – smashing Stan's knees. Stan's blood-curling scream reiterating the gruesome amount of pain he was immersed in.

"Oh shit!" Rager exclaimed as he instantly fired-up the Mustang's 429 engine.

"What do we do?" Luke asked, his voice shaking in fear.

Rager didn't answer. Instead, he unleashed 500 horsepower to his rear ties and lurched the car toward the mayhem just 100 yards in front of him.

As Stan attempted to emerge from the GTX, he raised his arms to protect his head from the raised shovel that was about to ascend onto his skull. As the shovel-wielding man was about to bring down even more pain to Stan, Rager's speeding Mustang slammed into his upper legs, sending him tumbling across the road, where Ralph was only beginning to shake off the daze of being clobbered with a steel shovel.

"You son-of-a-bitch!" Ralph yelled as he grabbed the loose shovel from the gutter.

"Go! Go! Go!" Rager yelled as he peeled out of the scene.

Looking into his rearview mirror, Rager saw Ralph raise the shovel over his head and slam it down into the man's face. Still groggy, Ralph then fell forward onto the man.

Rager stomped the gas pedal to the floor.

Like a prizefighter into his 15th round of battle, Ralph now staggered back to help Stan upright, then supported him as they stumbled for Ralph's '66 Chevelle that was parked in a nearby alley.

"My ankle's freakin' broke, Ralphie!" Stan cried as they made their way to the car.

Ralph loaded Stan into the passenger seat, then wobbled around to the driver's side – only falling twice. He fired-up the worn Chevelle SS and bolted from the scene.

Lying on the cold pavement in Highland Park, Rick Irwin struggled to get some air into his lungs. Blood was flowing from his gums and nose into the back of his throat. Choking-up blood, Rick blinked at the stars in the Michigan sky and drew a breath – for one final time.

"That was too scary, man!" Luke exclaimed as the Mustang blasted onto northbound I-75, unaware that Ralph had just taken Rick Irwin's life.

"Do you think that dude saw you coming?" Luke asked.

"Nope. He didn't see us at all," Rager assured him. "We came out of nowhere and he didn't turn at us once he hit that pavement."

"That's cool," Luke grinned with confidence. "We could have gotten into a lot of trouble for that."

"Yeah," Rager replied, "a lot of trouble."

* * * * * * *

Officer Harlan Boggs took another voracious bite from his ham sandwich as his police radio blurted out an APB. A thwarted auto theft attempt had left the car's owner beaten to death down in Highland Park. A dark Chevrolet had been seen racing from the area by the victim's wife – a mother of two children – after the violent row.

"Hmm," Boggs uttered as he chewed on his dry sandwich. "I wonder...."

* * * * * * *

Heading out of work, Alison Chambers chatted with her fellow bank teller, Sheila, as she headed toward her baby blue Pinto.

"Well, another day of survival at *Midwest Yank and Thrust*," Alison joked. "It's amazing how many branches have been robbed. I wonder why ours has been ignored?"

"Don't count us out yet. There are a lot of desperate people out there," Sheila answered. "Ever since the auto union strike started, lots of the local businesses have been letting people go. It's crazy!"

"I've only been here for a month and I already find myself sizing-up every man that walks through the front doors," Alison admitted. "You just never know."

Sheila changed the subject away from their hazardous daily grind.

"So…are you meeting your new beau tonight?" Sheila teased. "Or are you going to do that crazy jogging thing you do?"

"I need some time to get my head together," Alison replied. "I'm going to jog a few miles, then I need to visit my dad."

"Is everything okay?" Sheila asked.

"Oh yeah, everything's cool," Alison laughed nervously. "My father thinks like I do and sometimes I actually listen to his advice."

"Well that's different these days!" Sheila snickered.

"Besides," Alison admitted, "I was really bad this weekend. I smoked and partied and stayed up way too late."

"Oh no, not you!" Sheila giggled. "Miss Goody Two Shoes had a rough weekend!"

"Yeah, unfortunately," Alison winced. "It's all groovy. I'll get back on track by tomorrow.

"That running thing you do?" Sheila shook her head as she lit a cigarette. "That fad is gonna fade away as fast as it arrived – and that's why I'm not going out and spending my hard-earned money on those crazy-looking running shoes."

The two women parted ways and Alison sparked up her Pinto. As the four cylinders wound up, she shook her head.

"Should have got a Hemi," she sighed as she shifted the Ford into gear.

CHAPTER 14

Rager's Homecoming

Kent Rager swung his Mustang down the long row of dinghy tenement houses. If tasked to rename the street, one would be hard pressed not to call it *Ramshackle Way*. The houses were all painted in different colors – as long as they were brown. Stray dogs nosed through tipped garbage cans while paper trash swirled above like seagulls swarming a landfill. Street sweepers had ignored the gravel and salt that had been throughout the winter months.

Rager avoided this place as much as he could, but it was his old neighborhood and his father lived alone in the house he'd purchased when he was a young, proud autoworker – fresh from his country's victory over Nazi Germany.

Rager parked the Boss 429 behind his father's worn down '57 Ford Fairlane and scanned about the neighborhood to be sure the local thieves were nowhere to be found. He tossed his lit cigarette to the sidewalk as he carefully navigated the rotted planks on the front steps. Reaching above the window casing to his left, Rager retrieved a house key and entered.

"Hey Pops! You here?" Rager called out.

He navigated through the kitchen where filthy plates and empty boxes of Chinese take-out consumed every available inch of counter space. Beyond the kitchen was his father's favorite room, his man cave, or as he called it, *The Smoking Room*. It was there where Rager found his father – asleep on the couch a near-empty fifth of Shenley

Reserve whiskey, which his dad purchased in cases at a time whenever his UAW pension check arrived.

"Hey…Pops! Wake-up, man!" Rager demanded loudly. "C'mon, pop! Get the hell up!"

Karl Rager grunted, then wiped his hand on his soiled wife-beater shirt as he rolled toward the sound of his son's voice.

"What time is it?" Karl grunted as he reached for an empty pack of Camels. "Shit! I'm outta butts too."

Kent pulled his pack of Lucky Strikes out of his shirt pocket and tossed then into his father's lap.

"I hate these damn things," Karl protested.

"Then don't smoke 'em," Kent snapped back.

Avoiding any eye contact with Karl, Kent looked around at the nicotine stained walls and curtains, which was his father's entire universe – unless he decided to expend some of his energy to drive to the local market for food, cigarettes and another case of Shenley's whiskey.

"Dad, do you need anything?" Kent asked. "Do you want me to send that bag boy at the market down here with a box of food for you?"

Karl shrugged and reached for his open bottle of whiskey. "Yeah, I could use some grub," he shrugged. "And Camels too. I need a carton."

"You got it, Pops," Rager nodded as he lit another cigarette. "You'd better do some cleaning in that kitchen before the rats move in."

"Ahhhh, yeah, yeah," Karl scoffed. "It's a lil' late for that. Them dirty bastards rule the house at night."

Kent shook his head. "I'll send some rat poison with the groceries then. Just don't get hammered and try to eat it."

"You're real funny, kid," Karl waved him off with a scowl.

"Look, I paid your electricity and water bills, but you're gonna have to pay for your car insurance," Kent ordered. "Be sure to pay that as soon as you get your pension dough, okay?"

"Yeah, yeah. No worries, kid," Karl nodded.

Rager walked down the hall to his old bedroom. The twin bed mattress had been torn open by visiting rodents and the old magazine photos of Shelby Mustangs and Thunderbirds were curled and yellowed as they hung on the yellowed walls.

Rager pulled the twin bed aside just enough to free the area rug that it sat upon. He pulled the rug toward him, then lifted a loose floorboard. He reached down and pulled out a bulging, brown paper lunch bag.

Looking over his shoulder, Rager pulled a wad of cash from his jacket pocket and stuffed it into the bag.

"I'm gonna need another bag," he grinned through his cigarette.

Rager replaced the board, slid the rug back in place and dropped the twin bad back onto rug. He exited the room.

"Alright, them I'm outta here, Pops," Kent said. "You take care of yourself and I'll drop by next week, okay?"

But Karl had already grabbed his Zenith Flash-Matic TV remote and was tuning in to afternoon soap operas. He was transfixed on the television as Kent exited the room.

"Yeah, I'll see ya, Pops!" Kent called back sarcastically as he pushed open the front screen door.

In the driveway, Kent shooed away a handful of curious kids who were peering inside his Mustang.

"C'mon, you kids. Beat it!" Kent bellowed as they scattered down the alleyway.

* * * * * * * * *

Word on the street had spread fast about Rick Irwin's murder. Many had seen Irwin's '69 GTX prowling Woodward on a Friday night when he'd make his way north to find some fresh competition. Rick was a well-liked family man who worked long hours on a steel construction crew that serviced the four automakers. His only release was working on and running street competition in his GTX, but family came first with Rick, so he was never out racing on a Saturday night.

There were rumors around Big Boy's that it may have been Rager and his rag-tag team of thug grease monkeys who were caught in the foiled attempt to jack Irwin's car, but nobody was about to actually come out and ask Kent Rager, however the fact that Stan and Ralph hadn't been seen in days fed-in to these suspicions.

Denny Stark was convinced that it was the work of Rager and his goons and he couldn't wait to meet up with Alison and share that opinion, but like Rager and company, Alison had not been seen at Big Boys for a few days.

Denny would cruise the parking lot in his Roadrunner several times every evening, then cruise Woodward Avenue, hoping to see her powder blue Pinto somewhere on the strip.

Denny had swung by Tucker and Hoyt's shop and left the Roadrunner to be massaged with a fresh cam, an Edelbrock intake and a higher CFM Carter AFB. Hoyt had completed the work in a single day and Denny was very happy with the results.

When he wasn't searching for Alison, he was raking-in some pretty decent cash by reissuing challenges to cars that had previously beaten him. Denny's opponents thought it would be some easy money, until Denny shut them down. The winnings were handed over begrudgingly and Denny thoroughly enjoyed it.

"Payback's a bitch!" he'd laugh as he counted his winnings in front of the losing driver. "Let Steve Muller know I'm gunning for that '67 Coronet Hemi of his."

Denny's joy was short lived, however – he was beginning to worry about Alison's whereabouts and thought that she may have moved away to escape Rager's grasp. Or maybe Rager was holding her hostage somewhere. Perhaps Stan and Ralph had dumped her body into a lake.

Denny's mind raced faster than a speeding GT40, and his theories only made him even more anxious with each passing day.

* * * * * * * * * *

Alison pulled her Pinto onto a worn spot on the Chambers family's front lawn. The two tire tracks appeared after Alison had earned her driver's license and her father, Leonard, didn't have room in the driveway for a third Ford. As the grass wore out, Leo had covered the tire tracks with crushed stone, making it easier for his daughter to pull her '65 Falcon in and out under icy conditions.

Alison walked across the grass to the side entry of the big colonial-style house and entered.

"Dad? Mom? Anyone home?"

"We're out on the back veranda," her mother called back.

In the warmer months, Leo and Stephanie Chambers would move their single television set to the back porch where they'd eat dinner and watch the nightly news. Alison walked through the kitchen and onto the enclosed porch. The air was thick with cigarette smoke. In the background, Walter Cronkite was sweating under the CBS News studio lights as he described yet another day of conflict in Vietnam.

"You know," Alison quipped, "everybody in this entire neighborhood has a color TV now."

"Ah, who needs it?" Leo scowled. "It's just a big waste of money. I've heard them color sets only last about two years."

Alison's mom nodded. "We only watch the news and *Perry Mason* anyway."

"And once in awhile, we'll watch that crazy *Laugh-In* show," Leo added. "Buncha hippie pot smokers run that show, you can bet."

Alison approached her mother and slid a Salem Menthol from Stephanie's pack.

"Oh dear, I wish you wouldn't smoke!" Stephanie winced.

Alison scanned the smoke-filled porch and waved the smoke away.

"You're kidding, right?"

"What's on your mind, little girl?" Leo asked. "Oh, I checked the payroll records at the Dearborn plant and the only guy named "Rager" I found was a guy named Karl, but he's retired on a pension now."

"Karl Rager? Not Kent?" Alison asked intently.

"Yeah, Karl Rager," he'd worked the assembly line since he got back from the war. He was infantry – he even stormed Normandy on D-Day…June,1944."

"But no Kent. You're certain," Alison implored.

"Nope, no Kent," Leo countered. "I guess that boy's lying to you, little girl."

"Great," Alison whispered.

"How's work going?" Leo asked.

"Right now?" Alison rolled her eyes. "I'm a bank teller – been there almost five weeks. I'm ready to rip my hair out."

"You're doing very important work, little girl" Leo assured her.

"Uh, yeah…if you say so, Daddy," Alison shook her head and grinned.

"Would you like to stay for dinner?" Stephanie asked. "Stuffed cabbage!"

"No. No thanks," Alison replied as she blew out a flume of smoke. "I've got to go running. It'll clear my head."

"You can't smoke butts and run too," Leo scolded. "It don't work that way."

"I know," she agreed, "but they both relax me. I need that right now."

Alison's hand was shaking noticeably as she raised the cigarette to her lips.

"I *really* need that right now," she sighed.

* * * * * * * *

It was dusk as Kent Rager maneuvered his 500+ horsepower Boss 429 in through the door of a ratty old garage. The exterior hinted of abandonment, but lights from inside suggested otherwise. It was the typical hideaway one would expect for a small trio of thugs like Rager, Ralph and Stan. There they were safe from the intrusion of photographers from *Good Housekeeping* magazine.

Ralph lowered the door behind Rager's Mustang and locked it shut. His head was wrapped in gauze – a large bloodstain marking the spot where Rick Irwin had batted him with a steel spade shovel.

Emerging from his car, Rager was visibly upset, it was one thing to boost cars, but quite another to be an accomplice to murder.

Stan was sprawled on a ratty old couch with Ace bandages on both ankles and a bag of ice on one knee. Spread out copies of yesterday's *Detroit News* served as his makeshift blanket. One might find it hard to determine which was grubbier: the old couch or Stan.

"You assholes really put our nuts in a vice last weekend," Rager yelled loud enough for Stan to jump to a prone position on the couch.

"C'mon, Rage," Ralph protested. "That cat was trying to kill us dead! We were protecting ourselves. Self-defense… or something like that, you know?

"So you clobbered the poor bastard in the face with a shovel when he was down?" Rager barked. "The guy is dead, you morons! Had a wife and two kids too."

"He just woulda got back up and hit us again," Stan offered. "Or worse, he coulda seen our tag number and we'd be sittin' in a cell right now!"

"So you idiots decided that attempted auto theft charges were far less serious than murder?" Rager scoffed. "What kind of logic is that?"

"That's Ralphie's logic, Rage," Stan protested. "I was on the ground with busted up ankles."

"It doesn't matter who did what," Rager yelled. "We were all involved in the boost and now we're all accomplices to murder. At the worst, we're going to have to lay low for a few weeks."

"What about pay?" Stan asked. "We gotta eat and I'm almost outta cigs, man."

Rager reached into his pocket and pulled out a wad of cash. He separated some cash from the roll.

"Here's 50 bucks," he said as he tossed some bills into Stan's lap. "Get what you need, but walk or call for a ride. You'd better keep that Chevelle off the streets."

"Gotcha, Rage!" Ralph said. "Hey man, I really think Stan needs a doctor. His ankles are swollen like a couple of grapefruit."

"No doctors," Rager ordered. "They take one look at Stan's ankles and they'll be calling the pigs down on us."

Rager pulled a pack of Lucky Strikes out of his black coat pocket and lit up a cigarette. He tossed the pack into Stan's lap.

"These'll hold you guys over until Ralph can make a run to the store," Rager offered. "And Ralph, be sure to get that bandage off your head and put on a wool cap or something so you don't raise any suspicion."

"Hey Rage," Stan puzzled. "Who's gonna boost that 442 we had planned?"

"That's easy," Rager chuckled, "the kid."

"The kid?" Stan spat out. "He's only 17, man!"

"The kid's part of the business, so the kid's gonna help on a boost," Rager winked. "He'll drive the 'Stang and be my eyes while I jack the 442. We need to keep cash flow rolling."

"Good luck with that," Ralph laughed. "That kid's just a spoiled lil' rich boy."

"Not when I'm finished with him," Rager grinned as he blew out a plume of smoke. "He wants to be a tough guy? Well, I'll help him reach his dream."

Rager nodded toward the garage door and climbed back into his black beast. Ralph pulled the garage door open and waited for Rager to back out.

"Lay low," Rager nodded as he backed past Ralph.

"Hey, we're cool," Ralph said.

CHAPTER 15

Second Verse – Same as the First

Denny Stark's heart sank as he quickly scanned the Big Boy's parking lot for Alison's blue Pinto. He was going to pass through and head to the new McDonald's burger stand further up the strip, but decided to stay when he spied Hoyt's sublime green Duster 340. He pulled his Roadrunner in next to Hoyt's Mopar, secured the parking brake and headed toward the entrance.

Inside, the diner was abuzz as usual, but some of the excitement was toned to an all-time low as many were still discussing the death of Rick Irwin. Even Lenora seemed a lot less enthusiastic as she waited on the regulars – her smile was noticeably absent.

Denny scanned the booths until he spotted Tucker, Dawn and Hoyt hunkered into a corner booth. He made his way through the crowd and slid in next to Hoyt.

"I didn't hear any requests for permission to sit next to me," Hoyt said in his most deadpan tone.

"I don't have to ask anymore since you've eaten half my French fries every time I've sat with you," Denny joked. "My presence guarantees you more fries."

"Permission granted," Hoyt laughed.

"So what's hot?" Tucker asked as Lenora arrived with tall glasses of Coca-Cola.

"You mean, besides that murder last week?" Denny shook his head in disgust.

"It's so sad," Dawn interjected. "That guy had a family."

"Sounds like a Rager deal to me," Hoyt added.

Denny shifted uncomfortably in his seat.

"I'm a little concerned about that blond chick, Alison. You know, Rager's latest squeeze?" Denny prompted. "You guys know who I mean?"

"Yeah, we've seen her with Rager a few times," Dawn answered. "I've talked to her before. She seems cool. Very smart!"

"Beautiful girl," Hoyt added.

"Well, last week, I told Alison about Rager's car jacking escapades, you know?" Denny explained. "And right after that she just disappeared. Ain't seen her here or on the boulevard all week."

"Did you just use the word *escapade*?" Tucker joked.

"I'm serious here, Tuck," Denny countered. "She was pretty upset about it, but then I saw her with Rager on Friday night as they were leaving here. Ain't seen her since."

"Why are you concerned?" Dawn asked. "If you told her what a scoundrel Rager is, then she's probably avoiding the scene so he can't use his evil charms to seduce her again."

"Did you just use the word *scoundrel*?" Tucker grinned.

"C'mon, Tuck. Enough!" Dawn growled.

"Yes, ma'am!" Tucker saluted.

"So you've been worried enough about Alison enough to check on her whereabouts?" Tucker asked.

"Hmm... sound like someone's got a little crush goin' on," Hoyt quipped.

Denny blushed as he lowered his head.

"Yeah... I guess I do," he admitted. "I was just getting to know her when Rager swooped in with his dark charisma and stole her attention. But I saw her last week and warned her about Rager. Maybe I shoulda kept my big mouth shut."

"Yeah, for your own sake," Hoyt added. "Rager would have you pulverized into raw meat if he found out you exposed him to her."

"Raw sawdust!" Tucker added.

"Guys? Please? This is serious," Dawn winced.

"I ain't afraid of Rager," Denny shrugged, "or his two goons. But I'm afraid of what he can do to her. I mean, the guy's capable of anything if you piss him off."

"Look what he did to Tucker's GTO when he lost that race to him," Dawn reminded them. "If Sgt. Boggs wasn't there to shoot out his front tire we might all be dead right now."

Abruptly, Denny's eyes lit up. He stood up and looked out through the plate glass window.

Alison's powder blue Pinto was pulling into a parking spot just outside the entry doors.

"Oh my God!" Denny exclaimed. "She's here!"

"Stay cool, man," Tucker said. "You don't want to raise any eyebrows around here. Too many loose lips."

"I want her to know I'm here," Denny said excitedly. "It's really crowded in here!"

"Uh… I think she knows," Hoyt nodded as he motioned toward the window.

Alison was peering into Denny's Roadrunner, then turned and headed for the restaurant doors.

"Stay cool, Denny," Dawn laughed. "Why don't I go talk to her and invite her over?"

"Thanks, Dawn," Denny replied with a sheepish grin.

Tucker got up from the booth and allowed Dawn to slide out and weave through the crowd to meet Alison. Denny watched as the two greeted each other and exchanged a short hug. They made their way back to the corner booth.

"Well, look who slithered in here," Alison joked as she spotted Denny sitting in the booth.

Denny was tongue-tied, but was grinning from ear to ear as he stood to allow Alison to slide in between himself and Hoyt.

Lenora arrived just as they all settled in and already had two more Coca-Colas for the new arrivals.

"You kids all want the same thing?" Lenora asked as she set down some extra silverware wrapped in napkins.

"No fries for me," Alison replied. "Can I get a small garden salad with no onions?

"Wow! We have a health nut in here!" Lenora joked. "One side salad coming up."

"Are you really a health freak?" Denny asked – secretly wishing he hadn't asked the question as it left his lips.

"Why, is that bad?" Alison shot back, her face displaying some major concern.

"No, not at all," Denny's voice quivered slightly. "I'm just wondering. 'Never seen a salad ordered here before."

"I'm kidding you, Denny," she laughed. "Of course I'm a *health freak*, as you so delicately put it. It's the latest trend. People are going to start eating healthier, exercising and looking groovier than ever."

"I highly doubt that," Hoyt deadpanned. "Just a fad."

"Yeah, okay, Willy!" Tucker laughed. "This coming from a guy who predicted *The Doors* would be around forever!"

Everyone at the table laughed uproariously as Hoyt cowered into his corner of the booth.

"Well, well, well, that must have been *one* pretty damn funny joke! Anyone care to share it with me?"

The startled group looked up to see Kent Rager sneering over them.

As usual, Hoyt was the first to pounce back at Rager.

"Which sewer did you just crawl out of, Rager?"

"Clever, Mopar Boy," Rager grinned. "Have you raced your Dumpster 340 lately? I hear they have these new trikes called Big Wheels that you might be able to beat."

"What exactly do you want, Kent?" Dawn spat out angrily.

"Why, I'm just here to say hello," Rager said as he pasted a shallow smile on his expression. "Oh and I'm here to get my girl. I hope you all don't mind my spoiling the party by taking Alison away."

"Maybe she doesn't *want* to leave, chump," Tucker countered.

"Let's let her decide," Rager grinned. "I don't think she'd actually prefer your company, scrote."

"I don't see your two henchmen around anywhere," Tucker mocked. "Are they at your secret lair?"

"I don't need my *race coordinators* to assist me in taking my best girl out for a date," Rager said.

"A date?" Hoyt shot back. "Seems more like a kidnapping to me."

"Guys, guys," Alison said as he held her hands up. "Let's stop this foolishness, okay?"

All eyes were on Alison as she looked around at the gazes fixed upon her.

"Kent, please. If you want to talk to me, wait outside and allow me to enjoy my meal with my friends?

"You call these bottom-feeding *crustaceans* your friends?" Rager laughed.

"She's my friend, Kent!" Dawn interjected. "Leave her alone and let her eat her dinner."

"Did he just say *crustaceans*?" Hoyt joked – but no one was laughing.

"By the way, Mr. Village Burning War Hero, we have some unfinished business to take care of. Maybe this weekend up north of Crooks?

"Why should I race you?" Tucker answered. "You don't make good on your bets."

"Oh yeah, right!" Rager laughed. "You want my old burned-out Mustang? I can tell you where the wrecking yard is that it was hauled off to, although they probably crushed it by now. Even then, it could probably still beat that lead sled Pontiac of yours."

"Ha!" Hoyt guffawed. "You didn't beat Tuck the last time so what makes you think you can beat him with your Fix-Or-Repair-Daily Rustang?"

"Clever, Hoytie-Toytie," I'll bet it took you years to come up with that," Rager countered.

"Don't race him, Tucker," Dawn pleaded. "He's not worth the gas you'd burn to beat him."

"Don't listen to the common street whore in your midst," Rager sassed. "Her knowledge of cars doesn't extend beyond the view from the back seat cushions."

"Kent, stop!" Alison barked. "That is enough!

Rager stood and fixed a steely look upon Tucker.

"See you on Saturday night. North on Crooks Road, just south of Troy," Rager commanded. "It's a marked half-mile run on the right side and if you don't show? Well, let's just hope your street walker bitch is willing to share her tampons with you."

Alison slammed her napkin on the table and stood up.

"Look, I'm going to go, everyone," she begged apologetically. "The only way to stop this nonsense is for me to take this child out of here. I'm sorry and I hope he didn't ruin your evening!"

Denny stood and let Alison exit the booth, but Rager wasn't finished. He pushed Denny back a step and went nose-to-nose with him.

"That's my girl, Mr. Beep-Beep," Rager whispered angrily. "Take your Plymouth Load-runner and drive it off a bridge."

Again, Denny's mouth shifted into gear before his brain had fully engaged.

"I'll race you for pinks!" he blurted. "Saturday night… north of Crooks. I'll be there!"

"I wouldn't waste my time on a car that *Wile E. Coyote* could catch in his sleep," Rager laughed. "But I'll do you one better. I'll race the baby killer over here with his *Got Towed Off*, GTO and you, my friend… *You* will race my counterpart; the Purple People Eater."

"Don't do it, Denny!" Hoyt protested. "You will lose! That kid's crazy and his car is crazier!"

Denny looked at Hoyt, but testosterone overload was forcing his brain to shutdown. He looked at Alison, who only shrugged at Denny's dilemma.

"You're on, butthead," Denny responded. "Pinks, plus five hundred bucks to sweeten the pot!"

"Done!" Rager chuckled. "This is going to be an epic gain on my end. Now I just have to figure out where I'm going to have that Roadrunner chopped and sold, piece by piece."

"You'll need that Roadrunner to haul your ass around once I own that Mustang!" Tucker countered.

"Oh, Tucker, no!" Dawn cried out.

"It's okay, Dawn," Tucker assured her. "We'll enjoy a nice weekend away when I sell his Boss Mustang to a local charity for half price."

"Can we just go now, Kent?" Alison pleaded loudly.

Rager pushed out his arm in order to escort Alison from the restaurant, but Alison looked at him with contempt and breezed by him.

"Yeah, right…" she blurted as she rolled her eyes and stormed for the door.

Rager turned and nodded, "Enjoy your evening, gentlemen. Oh, and you too, Hoyt."

Rager smirked and followed Alison out.

"What just happened?" Dawn asked. "Are you guys nuts?"

"I feel the weight of the world upon my shoulders," Hoyt moaned.

* * * * * * * *

Almost out of breath, Harlan Boggs hobbled his large frame through the precinct front doors. With only two years left until retirement, an eight-hour shift in a hard-cushioned police cruiser was as punishing on his bones as an eight-mile jog. Climbing the fifteen granite steps to the precinct's front door was the day's final challenge.

Boggs wheezed slightly as he dropped a folder of fresh traffic violations onto the desk sergeant's counter.

Sgt. Dave Vernon had been assigned to night duty at the same desk for the past four years after an unfortunate mishap where he gave chase to a hopped-up '62 Biscayne that ran through the business district during rush hour. The damage to other cars and personal property was so extensive that the City of Royal Oak was still in litigation with business owners and injured pedestrians.

"Not too busy out there tonight," Boggs said. "Only a few wannabes and a couple of hardcore strokes. I spent more time chasing the pot smokers off the city hall steps."

Boggs plodded toward the stairway to descend to the basement locker room where he'd change into civilian attire so he could have a late night coffee and a slice of rhubarb pie at Nelly's Diner before heading home.

"Hey, Boggsy!" Vernon called to him. "We got a description of the car that boogied from that murder scene last weekend if you're still interested.

Boggs turned and lumbered back to the desk.

"Whatcha got?" he asked as he took a sheet of paper from Vernon.

"That getaway car was a mid-60s GM model," Vernon explained. "It was a dark red or maroon color and it was loud. The witness we interviewed thought it might be a Olds Cutlass or a Chevy Malibu. And it was dirty, he said. He claims it was still covered in road salt stains and had a dent in the rear quarter panel."

Boggs raised his eyes as he read the description, "Interesting," he nodded. "Thanks, Vern."

* * * * * * * *

It had been several days since Lucas Fischer had witnessed the ham-fisted boost-gone-wrong with Rager. Despite checking the parking lot at Big Boys a few dozen times, Luke was a warrior without his leader. He wasn't so wet behind the ears to be numb to the fact that Rager and his boys were laying low, but his ego still demanded that he push the locals into racing his Challenger by cajoling them until they became red-faced with anger and then Luke would press his 450-horsepower 440 six-pack into service.

While he wasn't making the big money that he enjoyed when Rager arranged the duels, he was content with simply beating his competitors and razzing them as he snatched the money from their hands.

However, without Rager, Luke was stumbling. He lost big one night on a lonely side road where he'd thrown-down against Chip Brown's '70 Hemi Cuda. Chip had removed all Hemi identification from the exterior sheet metal, so Luke was clueless about what he was getting himself into. A quarter mile strip that was marked-off on Interstate 75 was where Luke finally learned a lesson in humility; the Cuda had beaten him by a full car length... and then some. Luke forked over $100 and a huge helping of pride. Chip promised he was going to tell everyone that he'd beaten the plum crazy Challenger.

To add to Luke's problems, his nights on the strip were beginning to affect his grades. While his father was too involved with his executive chores at Chrysler, Luke's mother was beginning to see that Luke wasn't always going to the library or attending study groups. The plan was for Luke to become a Wolverine, yet despite his father's political influence; it was going to be a hard push to get him accepted. Luke was barely earning passing grades and he knew it was time to start using his racing cash to buy some test answers from the nerds at his Grosse Pointe private school.

But everything was about to change when Luke finally bumped into Rager's mechanic, Quentin Seymour. Quentin told Luke to meet Rager on Thursday night across the street from Big Boys.

While Luke was excited about racing for Rager again, Rager had other plans for his young apprentice.

* * * * * * * *

Rager teased the pedal of his Boss 429 and blurted out some raw horsepower notes that announced to anyone within earshot that he was still the king of Woodward Avenue.

Despite her knowledge of Detroit muscle, Alison remained unimpressed. She rolled her eyes and shook her head. She had decided to hold her cards close and not let Rager know what she knew. Alison was attempting to trap him in another lie, so there was no way she was sleeping with him until he either came clean or could explain why her dad, Leo was wrong about his employment at the Dearborn Ford plant.

Rager reached for Alison's left thigh and caressed it in his hand as they cruised east along Route 96. Alison felt a nauseating pit in her stomach, but didn't want to let on that she was repulsed by his touch.

"So… are we working tonight?" she asked in an attempt to keep things appearing normal.

"Nope. Off 'til Thursday night," Rager grinned. "I've got to meet the Challenger kid for a race I set up for him."

"You mean that high school kid?" Alison asked.

""Yeah, what about it?" Rager blurted back.

"Don't you think that boy could get hurt street racing?" she asked.

"Look, if I don't set up his races, he's gonna do it on his own anyway, you dig?"

"So you don't care if he gets hurt or killed in a car accident?" Alison probed, trying to set the stage for an intense disagreement – enough for an excuse not to go to the motel for the evening.

"Like I said, the kid's gonna race. Period." Rager asserted. "Why not make a nice piece of change off a crazy kid with a fast set of wheels?"

"Because you're an adult, Kent!" Alison protested. "That's why!"

"What the hell has gotten into you?" Rager demanded. "Did your brain get polluted with slop from those shitheads back at Big Boys?"

"They never spoke a word about this to me, Kent," Alison insisted. "I just see it for myself, you know – as an adult?"

"Ah c'mon, babe," Rager grinned in an attempt to lighten the thick air. "The kid's using the cash to help pay for his college expenses. He might be a little wild, but he's a pretty smart kid, you know?"

"So you just have to hope he survives the *Summer of Kent Rager* and then he'll be safely off to school again?

Rager breathed a sigh of frustration. "We're not staying at the motel tonight, are we?"

"Hardly," Alison answered.

"How about we drop this topic and go get some dinner?" Rager grinned again.

"Fine," Alison sighed.

Inside her head, Alison was fighting back every impulse to come out and accuse Rager of lying to her, but she sensed there was something else... something more sinister and darker that she wanted to uncover. To her, it was something more than just stealing cars.

The Speed Shop, Royal Oak, MI – 5:30PM

Tucker Knox glanced up from the front counter at the wall clock that had been hanging in the same spot since Alvin Knox first opened the doors to his eight bay mechanical service garage. Alvin had just returned from his final mission against the Japanese on Okinawa and had also met his future wife, Edie. Tucker wanted to replace the old clock, but it was a part of the dated décor of his dad's shop – even with the half-inch of brown shop dust that sat above its number 12. It was already 5:30 and Tucker was tired and hungry.

In the shop, Hoyt had his head buried under the hood of Tucker's '65 GTO.

"Hoyt! What do you say we call it a day and get our night started?" Tucker yelled.

"My night's already started, Tuck!" Hoyt called back. "When I finish your GTO, I can go home, take a shower, eat some grub and grab some sleep. Then I have Denny's Roadrunner coming in tomorrow night."

"Nice life," Tucker joked. "How do you plan to crank a 383 with enough grit to beat that kid's 440 Challenger?" Tucker puzzled.

"Well, we know Quentin put a cam in it, headers...the usual stuff," Hoyt explained, "but Denny just put in a Crane cam too, but the kid's intake is all stock, so that's where we're going to focus. Dual quads with an Edelbrock intake, plus I have a few other tricks up my sleeve."

"What about the Goat?" Tucker asked. "I know Rager's had Quentin work that 429 so it can actually breath again, so what are we doing to my 428?"

"Looks like your mill's days on the Trips are over, buddy," Hoyt shook his head as if he was in mourning for Tucker's tri-power set up. "I worked a deal out with Schornack to swap for a dual quad intake. I'll be changing out the three Rochesters for two gas-chug-a-lugging Holley four-barrels."

"How am I gonna handle all that?" Tucker asked. "My rears already break loose on the tri-power.

"Ah!" Hoyt raised a finger like a mad scientist and then motioned to a tarp near the back wall of the shop. As he walked quickly to the tarp he continued his lesson. "On thing I've noticed about Rager? He never pays attention to his rubber. By that I mean, he's running stock Mustang Boss 429 width tires."

Hoyt grasped the tarp and unveiled two mounted tires.

"Taa-daa! These, my good man, are Mickey Thompson racing tires. Not scrawny little eight-inchers… Oh no! These are 12-inch wide sticky slicks!"

Tucker's mouth dropped at the sight of the two racing tires.

"How the heck did we afford those?" he gasped.

"You know something?" Hoyt pondered with continued dramatic effect. "Those Chevy guys ain't such bad dudes after all. They sold 'em to me for cheap. Same bolt pattern on the wheels too. I like to call 'em "plug n' play!"
"Plug and play?" Tucker shook his head. "That's rich, man! I swear, the shit you come up with sometimes…"

"With the combined extra intake and fantastic traction, you already have an edge on Rager. Plus, you have all the Poncho god-given torque you could ever want in that 428. You're just going to need some speed toward the end of the run."

"And we do that... how?" Tucker frowned.

"Remember we talked about how cool it would be to make air dams and spoilers to make cars safer, but also faster?" Hoyt asked.

"Well, you... and Denny too, are gonna have air dams under your front core supports," Hoyt winked. "Nothing fancy, I'm just going to bolt up a v-shaped piece of heavy duty 8-inch aluminum roof flashing. Painted black, of course. They'll never spot it on Saturday night."

"So that directs air around the car instead of under it?" Tucker surmised.

"Egg- zactly!" Hoyt chuckled. "You and Denny are going to double wax every square inch of your cars. I want every surface to be as slick as Richard Nixon's hair. Those cars need to glide through the air."

"That'll help?" Tucker puzzled.

"If it helps a guy fly faster in his Piper Cherokee, it'll help a car that's booking along near the 100 miles an hour mark." Hoyt nodded. "Every advantage, Tuck. Every single thing factors in."

"What about weight?" Tucker asked.

"Rager relies on sheer grunt and so does the kid," Hoyt explained. "We'll do the usual, you know; back seats out, spare tire gone, floor mats out – as much as we can save."

"That means Denny's going to have to clean all those cups and burger wrappers out of his back seat floor," Tucker snickered.

"We'll be ready for 'em," Hoyt assured him. "The rest is up to you and Denny."

168

"Yeah and if Denny loses his car to that smug kid? Bye-bye Alison," Tucker said. "She won't consider going with a guy who was stupid enough to wager his ride in a race against a 17-year old kid."

"Uh… Tucker?"

"Yeah, Hoyt."

"You wagered your own pink slip against Rager. Again." Hoyt shook his head.

"Hmmm," Tucker pondered. "I 'spose I did, didn't I?"

CHAPTER 16

Tightening the Noose

Stan and Ralph were beginning to feel like their old grubby selves again; the swelling had gone down in Stan's ankles and Ralph's scalp was scabbing over nicely.

Ralph had just completed a run for cigarettes and beer and was stashing the bottles of brew into their mold-encrusted refrigerator.

"Hey man, you've gotta see this!" Ralph bragged to Stan as he closed the refrigerator door. He walked over to the couch with a brown paper bag to where Stan was carefully rolling a joint.

"What's in the bag?" Stan asked.

"Take a look at this…" Ralph beamed as he pulled a .38 Smith and Wesson revolver from the bag.

"Groovy!" Stan grinned with brown-tinted teeth. "How the hell did you get that?"

"Remember that guy we sold the 327 block to? I bumped into him at the market. I asked him for the 50 bucks he owed us and when he didn't have it, he offered me this fine piece of American weaponry."

"Cool, man," Stan said as he handled the gun. "Got any rounds with it?"

"Yeah," Ralph grinned, "a whole box of 100 hollow points. If the pigs come lookin' for us, I ain't going down without a fight."

"I'm gonna need one too," Stan said as he pulled a long draw off his joint. "We're brothers, man. I'll stand up with you!"

"We can't tell Rage though," Ralph warned. "He'll take them away from us."

Stan handed the joint to Ralph, who took a deep hit off it.

"Yeah, baby," Ralph exhaled. "We's armed and dangerous!"

"Badasses!" Stan echoed.

* * * * * * *

Kent Rager pulled a Lucky Strike from its pack and fired-up a cigarette. Thinking twice, he pulled out a second one and passed it over to Luke Fischer, who was afraid to refuse it, because it was Kent Rager offering it to him.

Rager flipped open his Zippo and lit Luke's cigarette. Luke coughed and held back a gag, yet pretended he was just as cool as Rager.

"I like that black leather jacket you've got on, man," Rager said as he eyed Luke's coat, which was identical to his.

"Thanks, Rage," Luke nodded – pleased that Kent had noticed.

"I have you lined up to race Billy Lardner's 428 Cobra Jet Torino," Rager said. "It should be an easy three-hundred split."

"The red one?" Luke asked.

"Yeah, the red Torino. It's a fastback," Rager answered.

"I already beat that snail a month ago," Luke snickered.

"Well, the snail ain't no snail anymore," Rager winked. "That snail got a full massaging from Quentin."

"You mean *our* Quentin?" Luke was confused.

"The Q-man doesn't just work for us," Rager answered. "He did a rebuild on the 428 and he is pretty certain we can still beat it. Q says Lardner's a putz who starts pissin' his pants when his speedo breaks 100 miles per hour."

"So even if he's ahead of me at the start, I can beat him when he gets shaky and lifts off the pedal after 100?" Luke grinned.

"Exactly, which is why I would only flutter the three bills if it was a one-miler," Rager explained. "Lardner wasn't going to take that challenge until I busted his balls in front of a few hippie chicks he was hitting on. Dumb shit wanted to impress the chicks, so he took the bet."

"Ha!" Luke laughed. "He's still going to have to face them when he loses!"

"You just have to hold steady below redline when you hit fourth gear," Rager explained. "With your gear ratio, you'll be at about 120. Just hold on 'til he chickens-out and you cross under that railroad bridge. That's the end marker."

"Got it, Rage!" Luke said enthusiastically.

"Okay. Follow me out to the strip," Rager ordered. "Let's get this done. Then I have one more job for you tonight."

"One more?" Luke asked.

"Yeah, no big deal," Rager winked. "It'll take less than an hour."

"Okay, Rage," Luke said with some suspect. "Whatever you need."

* * * * * * * *

Alison slid in behind Sgt. Harlan Bogg's police cruiser and sat on his rear bumper until Bogg's decided he'd had enough and pulled into a vacant lot off Normandy Road. Alison stepped out of her Pinto and waited for Boggs to emerge from his cruiser.

"Can I help you with something, or do you just enjoy tailgating police cars?" Boggs asked.

"Can we talk in private?" Alison asked. "Like in your car?

"Sure," Boggs shrugged. "You don't look too dangerous."

"You don't know the half of it," Alison replied.

Inside Bogg's car, Alison took out a cigarette.

"You don't mind, do you?" she asked as she rolled down her window.

"What's on your mind, young lady?" Boggs asked.

" I want to know what you know about a guy named Kent Rager," she answered. "Do you know who he is?

"What… are you kidding me?" Boggs laughed. "What do you need to know?"

"Everything," Alison asserted, "but allow me introduce myself.…

* * * * * * * *

Luke Fischer pulled his Challenger up to the painted line beneath a lone streetlight that marked the beginning of a one-mile run to a railroad bridge. In the distance, Billy Lardner's 428 CJ Torino could be heard as it approached. Behind the Ford, several dozen cars from Big Boy's were following him in. The cars swung to the left and right shoulders and shut off their headlights – as not to attract any attention from the neighboring farmhouses.

Kent Rager was the exception, pulling his Boss Mustang to the center of the road – directly behind the Challenger R/T and the 428 Cobra-Jet Torino. He stepped from his car sparked a cigarette and waited for the crowd to gather. Quentin Seymour exited the passenger side – obviously a fill-in for the missing Stan and Ralph.

Standing atop his door jam with his walking cane wedged into his armrest, Rager motioned the crowd toward him.

"We've all seen this duel between two *very* boss cars driven by two empty-skulled mental midgets," Rager announced. "But this time, Billy Laudner has dropped an ungodly amount of hard-earned cash into his Torino. My man Quentin has performed his magic on this car! So, this match is new again. Place your bets! The Q-man will accept your cash wagers."

"I've had my mitts on both these cars, know what I mean?" Quentin boasted.

Rager approached Luke and Billy.

"This run is from a dead stop to the railroad bridge which is exactly one-mile from that line," Rager explained. "There's no drafting allowed and if you see flashing lights behind you, we'll be doing our best to block the law from getting by us. So just get the hell outta here and meet up back at Big Boy's. Any questions?"

Billy looked a bit nervous. "Is still think we should have wagered for a half-mile," he said with some trepidation. "We'll be breaking the speed limit times two by the time we hit that bridge."

Rager raised his cane to the tip of Billy's nose.

"If you want to chicken out, then you can hand over your $300 and forfeit," Rager nodded. "Otherwise, get the hell into your damn car and experience what it feels like to be a man."

Billy turned and walked back to his car without a word. He climbed in and fired the beast to life. The sound coming from his headers and open pipes was threatening to Luke.

"Are you sure I can beat this dude?" Luke asked. "That car sounds like someone put a Tyrannosaurus Rex under his hood."

"I already told you how to beat this asshole, so just do what I tell you and you'll be $100 richer two minutes from now," Rager gruffed out a puff of cigarette smoke.

Luke headed for his Challenger and jumped in. Giving Rager a thumbs-up, he fired up the big 440.

The combined rumbling of both cars sounded more like an approaching squall and somewhere within earshot, a farmer was more than likely ushering his family down into a tornado shelter.

Rager spotted Dawn's friend Bernice sitting on the hood of her Chevy Nova in a pair of short shorts. He motioned to her, but Bernice shook him off. Rager called her again and she relented.

"Yeah, what do you want now, Kent?" Bernice asked as she popped her chewing gum.

"I'd like you to do the honors," Rager explained as he handed her a white handkerchief.

"Alright. Whatever," Bernice drawled in monotone. She'd started races before and it was no longer a thrill. "I don't even know why I come to these stupid things anymore."

"Judging by those shorts, you come to these stupid things to get laid," Rager quipped.

Bernice only smirked, turned and intentionally swung her hips in an exaggerated manner as she strolled toward the competing cars. The crowd of mostly males hooted and whistled as she strutted off. Bernice sauntered between the two rumbling cars and raised the handkerchief high. Pointing at each driver, she waited for a nod then let it go.

Abruptly, the gates of Hell opened up on the lonely country road as high-octane exhaust and white tire smoke combined with the sound of two roaring monsters. Bernice quickly disappeared into the cloud of smoke as the cars moved out. Seconds later, she emerged, fanning her face while choking.

"This was the last time, Kent!" she yelled. "I mean it!"

Rager was already too distracted to hear Bernice as he craned his neck to see who was taking the lead. From the sounds of the crowd yelling for Billy, he assumed Laudner was in the lead.

Luke Fischer was staring at the Cobra-Jet's taillights and he waited to jam his Hurst shifter from 3rd to 4th, but he was more concerned about his speed.

"C'mon, one hundred!" Luke yelled as he glanced down at his speedometer.

As he made a smooth shift into 4th gear, he saw the gauge hit 85 MPH.

"C'mon bridge!" screamed Billy Laudner as he too glanced down at his speedometer. He was at 90 MPH, but the railroad bridge was still a half-mile off.

Lucas began toying with the idea of running his engine beyond redline. He trusted Rager, but he wasn't used to seeing his opponent's taillights. As he approached 100 MPH, he made a spilt decision to stay below redline and believe that Billy would soon be lifting. Inside the Torino, Billy was pleading with his speedometer as the car began shuddering. The sound of the high-velocity air passing by his Ford was beginning to scare him. His windshield wipers both popped upward an inch or so as the air pushed on them.
Billy was beginning to lose his cool.
Luke checked his speedometer; the car was now passing the 100 MPH mark and creeping toward 105.

"C'mon, Billy!" Luke yelled. "It's time to start shitting your pants!"

"Billy cried out in fear as he gripped the steering wheel. He was approaching 110 mph – faster than he'd ever driven before, but his nerves were frazzled and his car was shaking even more.

With the bridge less than 200 yards away and the Challenger right on his tail… Billy lifted.

"Shit!" he screamed as he banged on his steering wheel. "I can't believe this!"

A bright purple phantom flashed by him as he heard his 428 engine winding down. Billy hit the gas again and shot under the bridge at 95 MPH, but the damage was done – Luke's Challenger was already slowing to make the u-turn back. Billy downshifted and applied his brakes. Sliding up to Luke's window, he came to a stop.

"What happened to you," Luke teased. "I thought you had me! Engine give out?"

"No. No. Nothing like that," Billy grinned sheepishly. "My brain gave out."

Luke's eyes widened as he looked back down the one-mile strip. At the far end, police lights were flashing and cars were quickly exiting the area.

"Holy shit!" Luke cried. "The pigs, man! Come on, let's boogie outa here! See you at Big Boy's!"

Luke swung his Challenger around behind Billy and both cars bolted from the scene.

* * * * * * *

Harlan Boggs exited his patrol car and calmly approached Kent Rager with the typical cop swagger. He glanced around before sliding a nightstick into his belt.

Rager eased up on his front fender and pulled out a cigarette.

"It's funny how everyone seems to disperse whenever I show up at these events," Boggs joked.

"It beats me," Sergeant Boggs," Rager replied. "We were just about to have a dance party and grill some hot dogs."

"Sure you were, Rager," Boggs laughed. "But you know what really puzzles me?"

"What's that?" Rager breathed out a hail of smoke.

"Well, normally if you were going to sit here on your car, you'd be accompanied by Larry and Curly," Boggs squinted. "Now why on earth would the stooges skip a fine cookout and music party out in the countryside?"

"I guess they must've had plans," Rager shrugged. "They're very independent thinkers."

"Not from what I've seen," Boggs volleyed back. "They're usually stuck to you like maggots on dog shit."

"Oh, those guys," Rager waved off Boggs. "They're like little kids, you know? Always late – always goofing off somewhere."

"You know what's even funnier?" Boggs asked.

"What's that, sir?" Rager asked.

"I haven't seen them at all lately," Boggs shrugged. "In fact, they seemed to have disappeared ever since a dirty, mid-sized Chevy with loud mufflers hightailed it from a boost gone bad on a GTX. This guy, Rick Irwin, was bludgeoned to death with a shovel. You hear about that?"

Rager felt a cold chill stun him to the core, but tried to remain cool, even though Boggs seemed to be onto Stan and Ralph.

Rager raised his cigarette to his mouth and took a long drag.

"Yeah, I heard," Rager said.

"You nervous, Rager?" Boggs asked.

"No, why?" Rager shook his head.

"Your hand was shaking as you took a drag off that butt," Boggs asserted. "Is there something you want to tell me? Maybe something that'll keep your ass out of jail?"

Rager shook his head. "Nope. Nothing's bothering me. I think I'm just worried about dear ol' dad."

"Oh yeah," Boggs cracked. "Is that the same dear ol' dad who never once visited you while you were in traction after your accident? Is he the same guy who wouldn't come to the door when I went to his house to inform him that you'd been in a car wreck? *That* dear ol' dad?"

Rager took another drag from his cigarette and stared off across the open field.

"With all due respect, that shit's my business, officer," he said.

"I'm gonna find out who, what and why and then I'm going to start making arrests," Boggs said, having suddenly become more aggressive. "And your little sidekick... your shithead-in-training? I'm going to hang him too. I don't care who his daddy is!"

Rager shrugged and stared off into the distance again as Boggs drew his nightstick. Boggs swung the stick and smashed the Mustang's front right headlight.

"By the way, you've got a headlight out," Boggs chuckled. "Better get that fixed before I have to issue you a citation."

"Thank you, Officer Boggs," Rager smiled sarcastically as he fought his inner temper.

Boggs climbed into his cruiser and fired it up. He swung close to Rager and leaned out his window.

"If I find out who just raced here tonight I'm taking both their licenses and cars," Boggs winked as he pulled away.

* * * * * * * *

Rager pulled into Big Boy's where Luke Fischer was holding court in the parking lot, but the only difference between his version was that he was being met with a chorus of boos and hisses with each bragging statement.

Rager waded through the crowd, pushing people aside in order to get to the core, where Luke was telling everyone about his big win.

"Let's go," Rager ordered.

"But Rage, I have an audience, just like you!" Luke protested.

"You're pissing them off," Rager said quietly. "Did you get the three bills from Billy?"

"Yes, Rage. He already split."

"Let's get out of here," Rager said quietly. "Get into my car."

"But what about my....?"

"I said get in my car!" Rager demanded.

Luke walked off to Rager's Mustang.

"Nothing to see here," Rager grinned and he addressed the crowd. "The kid did good, but he has to go home to do his homework!"

The crowd laughed and began to disperse as Rager headed for the Mustang.

180

With a blurp of throttle, the Boss 429 lumbered through the lot and out onto Woodward Avenue.

* * * * * * * *

Tucker pulled Dawn's Galaxie to the edge of the grass parking area over-looking Detroit.

"We've got to stop meeting like this," Dawn joked with some exaggerated drama.

"You know? I really think you're just using me for sex," Tucker winked.

"Oh, right," Dawn laughed. "Do you know how many guys proposition me every day at the record store?

"Actually, I don't," Tucker replied, "and I really don't want to know."

"So what is Hoyt up to tonight?" Dawn asked.

"He's toiling away on the cars," Tucker chuckled. "There's no way he'll allow Rager or the Fischer kid to beat us."

"That boy needs a girlfriend," Dawn said as she snuggled up closer to Tucker.

"What about Bernice?" Tucker asked. "She's ready to go with just about any guy who looks at her twice.

"Don't be mean, Tuck," Dawn laughed. "She's my best friend. I know she's a little loose, but who can blame her? She's bought into that whole "free love" movement going on."

"Yeah, free crabs too!" Tucker laughed.

"You are so mean!" Dawn said as she gave Tucker a playful punch.

"Hoyt has had a crush on my mother for years," Tucker said. "He doesn't think I've noticed, but when he visits my house, he gets all giddy and foolish around my mom.."

"So that explains why he doesn't chase women!" Dawn exclaimed. "He's smitten!"

Tucker took a deep breath as he took in the view in front of him. The glimmering stars above the city enhanced the city lights and illumination from Tiger Stadium. In the distance, the intermittent sounds of roaring V8s and screeching rubber could be heard.

Detroit was at the very apex of success, marketing beautifully designed cars with gobs of power and a population that was still not willing to accept Japanese imports due to still-fresh memories of the horrors of World War II.

"I'm scared," Tucker admitted.

"What, you? Scared?" Dawn puzzled. "You've been to Vietnam and back."

"I have too much to lose," Tucker explained. "The GTO, the business and maybe even you."

"You're not gonna lose me, so put that one to rest," Dawn grinned, "but your business?"

"If we lose, everyone will think we can't get it done," Tucker shook his head. "They'll take their cars to Quentin, or Schornack or anyone else but us."

"So you'll lose business if Rager and the kid win?"

"Street racers are a funny breed," Tucker said. "If they can't wrench them on their own, they'll ask around for the best shop. They rely on word-of -mouth."

"Wow," exclaimed Dawn. "I've never looked at it that way."

"Rager knows this. It's why he's always pushing Hoyt and me… and now Denny. He knows he can cripple the business."

"Is that all?" Dawn sensed there was more.

"Nope… there's more."

"And…?"

"I'm afraid I'll get hurt. If I can't work we'll lose the business. If I flip the car I'll not only lose, but I'll be paying hospital bills forever."

"Well, well, well, look who's growing up!" Dawn smirked. "You're finally growing out of your immature street racing phase!"

Tucker could only agree – he wasn't done with racing, but he wanted it on safer terms – like at the local tracks, where safety was just as important as speed.

"We need to advocate safer racing," Tucker admitted. "This dual match should have been run at Detroit Dragway on 5-dollar night.

"Maybe it's time to do what we talked about," Dawn asserted. "Promote safe racing. Heck, even Boggs will be on your side!"

"Yeah, maybe it's time…" Tucker shook his head as he came to grips with his new reality; he was now a business owner and part of the Royal Oak community.

"It's time for something else too," Dawn grinned.

"What's that?" Tucker puzzled.

"It's time for you and me to express our love for each other," Dawn explained. "It's why we drove all the way up here, isn't it?"

"Right," Tucker nodded as he leaned toward Dawn and kissed her. "Let's express ourselves!"

* * * * * * * *

Luke Fischer peered over the steering wheel of Rager's Boss 429 Mustang. While he felt fortunate enough to be one of the few who'd ever done so, he was also terrified: only 100 yards in front of him, Rager was using a slim jim to pop the driver's door lock on a brand new 1971 Olds 442.

Unlike Stan and Ralph, Rager was the consummate professional. He pulled up on the slim jim and was into the 442 in a matter of seconds. Screwing a slide hammer into the ignition column took a mere 10 seconds and popping the ignition lock was done an instant later.

Rager jammed a screwdriver into the open steering column and the car's engine erupted with a low, menacing burble. Rager engaged the floor shifter and swung the car out onto the street. The entire boost was done in less than 45-seconds and nobody had come out with a shovel.

Luke shifted the Boss 429 into gear and eased it out of the shadows to follow Rager.

Lucas Fischer – college bound and destined for a brilliant future – was now a felon – a bonafide car thief.

* * * * * * * *

Alison Chambers gripped a pencil between her teeth as she scrolled through the *Detroit News* microfiche on a public library monitor. With her long golden locks pulled back in a bun and her thick horn-rimmed glasses, she looked more like a library employee.

She stopped and squinted at an article. "Oh yeah, here we go," she whispered.

The headlines were in bold black, "Montrose Man Suffers Near Fatal Accident."

Alison began feverishly scribbling notes on a small pad. She was putting together a jigsaw puzzle of Kent Rager's profile. And if Sergeant Boggs came through with his arrest file, Alison would have a better understanding of whom she was dealing with.

One tidbit that Boggs had thrown her way was that area car thefts had dropped measurably as soon as Rager was hospitalized.

Her attraction for Rager the thug had been reduced considerably, but her curiosity and intrigue with him was now aroused. Despite what her heart was telling her, Rager's dark side was strangely appealing to her heart.

"Why do I always fall for the bad guys?" she questioned in her mind.

CHAPTER 17

The Edge of Insanity

The area was old and abandoned industrial park with less curb appeal than a 70-year old prostitute. The buildings were boarded up tight to keep out vagrants and rodents – even stray dogs avoided entering the park. Paint peeled from the old wooden windows and steel doors, while the courses of mortar and red brick on the exterior walls rose and dipped like a rollercoaster.

Kent Rager honked the horn twice, followed by a short beep in front of an old garage door. This was Dirk Sturgis' chop shop. As the door quickly raised, amber light and loud noise emitted out from the busy garage.

Rager pulled in the 442 and the doorman waved Luke in behind him. No cars were to be seen outside the building for obvious reasons.

The door was quickly closed behind them.

Inside the shop was busy a busy place, with metal grinders, air ratchets and acetylene torches burning through Detroit steel. The air was thick with smoke and sparks illuminated the dingy, poorly lit garage. It was said that Dirk Sturgis' chop shop could make an entire car disappear in under four hours.

Luke began to open the door to exit the Boss Mustang, but was rudely pushed back into the car by the doorman.

"You stay right where you're at, lil' fella," the doorman said through nicotine stained teeth. "You got no business here."

Rager exited the 442 as Sturgis approached. As customary, Dirk ignored Rager as he sized-up the Oldsmobile. After touching all the bases as he circled around the 442, Sturgis nodded with approval.

"You finally brought me something I can work with," Sturgis said. "W-30, automatic tranny, low miles and not even a ding."

"We aim to please," Rager smirked as he lit another cigarette.

"I'll give you twenty-two for it," Sturgis offered. "Not a bad haul for your five minutes invested in boosting this beauty."

"How about twenty-five?" Rager pushed back. "If it's so perfect, I should be paid for bringing in some premium steel."

Dirk pretended he didn't hear Rager as he walked across the garage to his office.

"Come get yer twenty-two hundred!" Sturgis yelled without looking back.

Luke craned his neck from the Mustang's window to take in the scene around him. He was amazed at how much activity could take place behind the doors of an abandoned factory.

Rager returned, flipping through his wad of freshly earned cash.

"I had a good night," Rager smirked as he flipped a few one-hundred dollar bills at Luke. "One's for the race you won and the other's for helping me on this boost."

Luke looked down at the cash in his hand.

"I made two-hundred bucks for a 40-second race and a one-minute car theft?" he beamed. "I could do this every day, Rager!"

"Cool your jets, kid," Rager said as he fired up the Boss Mustang's engine. "My two lunatics will be back in circulation as soon as the heat dies down."

Luke didn't hear Rager, he was 17-years old and had just earned more money in two hours than his classmates made working eighty hours bagging groceries at the local supermarket.

* * * * * * * *

Hoyt looked up at the shop wall clock. It was now 1AM and he was exhausted. He stepped back to look at the shining GTO and Roadrunner.

"You ladies each have a big task ahead of you, but I'm confident you're both as ready as ready can be," he said. "I've done all I can to make you the fastest cars to ever cruise the Woodward strip, but now it's up to you to finish the job. There's a lot at stake here, ladies. If your drivers keep their cool, don't mis-shift you and get off the line faster than their opponent, you will prevail!" he proclaimed loudly to the empty garage. "Make me proud, my precious ones. Make me happy."

Hoyt didn't hear the sounds of approaching footsteps as he concluded his speech and as he turned, he was met with a roundhouse punch to his left eye. He fell to the floor like a sack of Speedy Dry and through blurred eyes, he saw Rager's two filthy thugs, Stan and Ralph hovering over him.

"I never seen someone talk to a damn car before," Stan laughed as he belched out a combined aroma of beer and cigarette smoke.

"I never seen a guy talk to two cars at once!" Ralph chided back. Both hoodlums laughed uproariously at their stupid joke.

"What the heck?" Hoyt whined as he wiped blood from the corner of his eye.

"We got some advice for you and your boss man," Stan warned. "You best not win on Saturday night or there might be some major trouble. Know what I mean?"

"Yeah, we weren't around last time," Ralph recounted. "But this time, you're gonna see some shit go down if Rage or the kid lose that race."

"Ha! You two jailbirds missed the last race!" Hoyt mocked them – ignoring his own better judgment.

"But this time we'll be there," Stan warned. "And it ain't gonna be pretty."

Ralph stepped forward and pulled his revolver out, placing it on Hoyt's forehead.

"This ain't no idol threat!" Ralph barked.

"Did you just say *idol* threat?" Hoyt couldn't resist – even with a gun trained on his forehead.

"You just shut yer damn mouth!" Stan scowled as he kicked Hoyt in the chest.

"If you tell anyone…or you go to Boggs, you're gonna be wishing you'd never met Kent Rager, understand?" Stan exclaimed.

"What do you want me to do?" Hoyt gasped – out of breath from the kick to his ribs.

"You make sure them two cars are fast, but not too fast," Ralph grinned through green teeth. "Otherwise, you'd best disappear from Woodward Avenue."

"Yeah, or disappear from the whole state of Michigan!" Stan laughed.

"Okay, okay," Hoyt nodded as he tried to stand. "We don't need any trouble or violence. I'll detune the cars."

"You better not be lyin'," Stan sneered, "or it'll be the last race you ever see!"

Ralph walked over to the GTO and took aim at the front quad carburetor.

"No! No! Don't do tha…." Hoyt yelled, but it was too late.

Ralph squeezed the trigger and shot directly at the Holley carb, but rather than doing damage to the intake, the bullet ricocheted off the carb body and slashed through Stan's right ear.

"Yeeeeoooow!" Stan screamed. "You dumbass! Look what you went an' done!" Stan held his ear as blood poured from a torn lobe.

"Ah, it ain't nothin'," Ralph winced as he saw the blood. "It's just a scratch… a deep one"

Stan and Ralph moved for the exit door and were gone in an instant.
Hoyt stood and rubbed his ribs.

"I'm going to find a way to make these two birds even faster," he nodded with determination.

* * * * * * * *

Alison sprinted up the concrete stairs of the Montrose high school football stadium. She was wearing the new Adidas training shoes that were the current rage. Her grey sweatpants and matching sweatshirt made her look a bit like Rocky Balboa as she pushed herself hard for the top of the bleachers.
She stopped and turned as she caught her breath. From her point of view, looking out on the setting sun over Montrose, it was hard to believe that such a pristine, all-American township could be home to such evil maniacs as Rager and his two misfit goons.
Alison turned and jogged down the stairs. She made a final sprint to the parking lot to her car. Gone was the baby blue Pinto. Alison climbed into a new, slate gray '71 Ford LTD. After lighting a cigarette, she reached beneath the seat for her keys (remember those days?) and fired-up the 351 engine. She grinned at the sound of tuned dual exhaust.
It was time to head to Big Boy's for some dinner.

* * * * * * * *

Kent Rager scanned the lot at Big Boy's for Alison's Pinto. He decided to go inside to eat by himself – hoping she or (God-forbid), Luke, might arrive soon.

The diner became eerily quiet as Rager made his way to an open booth, then a low buzz followed. The entire diner was talking about the Saturday night duel.

"All by yourself tonight, Kent?" Lenore asked as she arrived to take his order.

"Not for long, I hope," Rager smiled politely.

As Lenore moved off, Rager spied Alison as she crossed the lot to the front door of the diner.
Alison slowly made her way through the crowd and sat down across from Rager.

"No more sitting next to me, huh, babe?" Rager shook his head.

"I don't know, Kent," Alison answered. "There are too many unanswered questions. I can't allow myself to be involved in anything that counters the law."

"What the hell are you talking about?" Rager asked. He was trying hard to conceal his temper.

"Well, for one... street racing," Alison answered. "I find it hard to believe that a man of your intelligence races illegally on the street."

Rager shook his head as he looked at his hands.

"It's not about racing," Rager explained. "It's about the cash. I can make more in 2 nights of racing than I can make busting my ass for forty hours at the Dearborn plant."

Yeah? Well, that's another thing," Alison sighed. "My dad is a payroll accountant at The Rouge. He can't find any record of your working there. Unless your name is Kirk."

"Kirk's my dad," Rager answered. "He worked there since he got back from the war. He made it to work every day, despite being a filthy drunk."

"But *you* didn't work there," Alison reiterated. "There's no record of you, Kent."

"It must be some sort of clerical error," Rager lied. "They probably pulled my file for workman's comp."

Alison stared into Rager's eyes, yet he never blinked.

"This guy is good," Alison thought. "The perfect liar."

"So… is there anything else that's eating at your pretty little head?" Rager chuckled.

"Yes. I don't like the idea of you working in a place that chops up stolen cars," she said. "Those cars are owned by hard-working people. They need them to get to work, to visit a parent in the hospital or to take their kid to school or the doctor."

Rager bit his lip – trying not to explode on Alison.

"I already told you it's temporary," Rager explained. "The money is good there too. I want to own my own new car dealership someday. I want to be legit."

"So you're willing to throw the dice that you don't get busted?" Alison asked.

"You've got to reach out and grab what's yours," Rager answered. "If the end justifies the means…"

"Good lord, you're impossible!" Alison shook her head. "If you want to continue our relationship, I want you to cancel tomorrow night's race with Denny and Tucker."

"That's some far out talk, right there, babe!" Rager laughed. "If we win this match up, not only will I have big money challenges coming from all over southern Michigan, but I can broker work for my mechanic, Quentin. I can pull a nice 10% off the Q if he becomes the speed guru of Royal Oak."

"It's all about money with you, isn't it?" Alison asked with some degree of anger. "Is there anything else I need to know about you?"

"Yeah babe, I'm good in the sack! Wanna try again?" Rager laughed.

"I don't think so," Alison winced. "You're such a dark, handsome man. It's a shame you can't see what you're doing is wrong."

"If you leave me, you'll be sorry," Rager warned.

"Is that a threat?" Alison asked.

"Nope. Not a threat," Rager said as his dark eyes pierced into Alison's soul. "I'll be successful one day and you'll be sorry."

Alison didn't believe Rager's explanation though. She knew what he really meant and it scared her to her bones. She tried to remain cool as she began to slide from the booth.

Rager grabbed her wrist.

"You're my girl. Got it?" Rager said through gritting teeth. "Stop this stupid shit about what I do for a living. It doesn't concern you. Just accept that I'm as wild as that Boss Mustang that I drive. Can't you do that?"

Alison feigned a smile and looked into Rager's eyes with as much affection as she could muster.

"Let me sleep on that, Kent," she smiled. "Maybe you're right."

With that, Rager released his grip on Alison's wrist.

"Are you going to have dinner with me?" he asked.

"Oh no, I'm sorry, I can't," Alison replied. "I promised my parents I'd stop by for dinner."

Rager stood as Alison exited the booth. He pulled her in tightly then kissed her on the lips.

"We'll be okay, babe. I promise," Rager nodded.

"I know," Alison said as she turned and left Big Boy's.

* * * * * * * *

Denny Stark practically leaped from Hoyt's Duster 340 as it rumbled to a stop outside Tucker and Hoyt's speed shop. He couldn't wait to get behind the wheel of his bored and stroked, dual quad Roadrunner and drive it to work. He grabbed the door to the shop to pull it open.

"Geez, Denny, let me unlock it first," Hoyt laughed.

Denny finally noticed the dark swelling and bruise on Hoyt's left temple.

"What the hell happened to you, man?" Denny asked with concern.

"Oh, you know," Hoyt attempted to lie, "the old *walk-into-the door-jamb-in-the-dark* thing?"

"That looks a lot worse than walking into the edge of a door," Denny answered. "Wanna try again?"

"That's my story," Hoyt said.

"Okay, man. That's groovy if you wanna play it that way," Denny shook his head.

Inside the shop, Denny sprinted to his Roadrunner. He deliberately dove onto the hood to give his car a hug.

"You are certifiably nuts!" Hoyt laughed as he pulled the keys from the shop board.

Denny grabbed the keys and jumped into the Roadrunner.

"Give it a few pumps on the pedal before you turn the key," Hoyt advised.

Denny pumped the gas and fired the big engine to life. The rumble from the car's exhaust would invoke fear into any potential challenger... or Challenger.

"Don't push her too hard," Hoyt warned. "Let everything get broken-in before you shoot for Mach 1 speed. Put some miles on her before tomorrow night's big win."

"Thanks Hoyt!" Denny yelled from the car.

Hoyt pulled open the garage door to unleash the Roadrunner.
"See you tomorrow night" Hoyt beamed as the car passed by him.

Tucker was arriving as Denny drove from the lot. He exited his dad's old pickup truck and pulled out his dad's old leather briefcase. Whether he needed it or not, Tucker always brought the worm brown briefcase home with him each night. It also made him look and feel more like a local businessman.

"He looks happy!" Tucker called out to Hoyt, who was rolling out a rack of new tires to display in front of the shop.

"Why shouldn't he be?" Hoyt answered. "He's got the hottest car on the strip!"

"Second hottest, you mean, right?" Tucker winked.

"Yeah, yeah. Second hottest," Hoyt laughed.

"What the hell happened to your eye?" Tucker asked.

"Brother? We've gotta talk," Hoyt said as he put his arm over Tucker's shoulder and walked to the front office door.

* * * * * * *

Alison Chambers adjusted her ear protection and raised a .45 semi-automatic to eye level. She fired-off nine straight rounds, then retrieved her target.

Every score was within 4-inches of dead center on the target. Three of those were direct hits at the core of the circle.

Ned Wright, the owner of the target shooting range, happened to be passing by.

"You're becoming quite the sharp shooter, Miss Chambers!" said Ned. "I've never seen a lady handle a .45 like you do!"

"Thanks, Ned, but that was only at 60 feet." Alison shrugged. "It just takes a lot of practice."

"Keep up the good work, young lady!" Ned nodded with approval.

Alison loaded a second clip and spun the wheel to move the next target to 75 feet. She took aim and…

* * * * * * *

Kent Rager blew his horn at the rotting red door at Ralph and Stan's auto shop. Ralph pulled the door open and Rager pulled the Mustang in.

196

"Quentin's on his way here," Rager said. "He's going to set my timing and make a few carb adjustments. I want you guys to pull the passenger seat, the back seat and even my radio. We'll be ready for tonight."

Another horn blast echoed through the garage. Outside, Lucas Fischer's Challenger R/T awaited entry. Stan pulled the garage door open again to allow the Dodge into the shop.

"This is gonna be one groovy night!" Luke called out as he exited his Challenger.

"Did you guys get at those cars in Tucker and Hoyt's shop?" Rager inquired.

"Nope. We couldn't," answered Ralph. "That bastard Hoyt was there all night. We busted in and gave him a pretty good warning though!"

"What did you do?" Rager asked.

"We just roughed him up a bit," Stan answered. "Put the fear of God into him!"

"So he cut your ear open in the roughing up?" Rager asked as he noticed the bandage on Stan's ear.

"Nah! Ralphie did that," Stan laughed.

"How did Ralph cut your ear open?" Rager asked again.

Ralph and Stan looked at each other, then went silent.

"Hoyt did it!" Ralph blurted out. "That little bastard Hoyt got a good punch in!"

Stan only nodded and began crawling into Rager's Mustang to remove the rear seat. Rager looked over at Luke and shook his head.

* * * * * * * *

Denny looked into his rear view mirror at the gray Ford LTD that was flashing its headlights at him. He kept on driving his Roadrunner until he saw the LTD wasn't backing off.

"You've gotta be kidding me," Denny laughed. "This Ford wants to run me?"

Denny pulled into the right lane, allowing the LTD to pull along side his Roadrunner. At the next light, the LTD stopped, and Denny was shocked to see Alison roll down her window.

"What happened to that cute lil' Pinto?" Denny asked.

"It's underpowered" Alison laughed. "I'm fixing that!"

"I see," Denny nodded.

"Meet me at the donut shop up ahead?" Alison asked.

"No problem!" Denny was happy to oblige.

The two cars pulled into the donut shop. Denny and Alison went inside and sat at the counter.

"So, to what do I owe this chance encounter?" Denny asked.

Alison took a sip of her coffee as she thought about her plan of attack. Instead of tip-toeing around the subject, she decided to just lay it out for Denny.

"I want you to cancel your race tonight," Alison said.

"You can't be serious!" Denny laughed. "I've got this covered... thanks to Hoyt, of course."

"Do I look like I'm joking?" Alison asked.

In his mind, Denny was weighing-up his need for speed and the fame of beating Luke Fischer versus his adoration for Alison

"Why?" Denny asked.

"Well, because "A" it's illegal? And "B" you might get hurt or killed?" Alison reasoned.

"But what do *you* care?" Denny asked.

Alison hesitated again. She didn't want to show her cards yet, but she reasoned that it was time.

"I care about you, Denny," she admitted. "Things didn't work out with Kent and me. He's very dangerous, so I want you to stay away from Rager and his thugss. Let's go have dinner in the city tonight."

"Wait a second," Denny answered, "you care about me? How much do you care?"

"I care about you enough where I don't want to see you get hurt, be attacked or even just lose your driver's license!" Alison reasoned. "There's a lot more at stake here than you realize."

"If I do race," Denny grinned. "Would you still consider having dinner with me?"

Alison made Denny wait for her answer. She bit into a pastry, then took a sip of coffee.

"Maybe," she grinned.

"Look, Alison, I have to race. I can't back down. I'd be the laughing stock of the entire strip," Denny explained. "Do you understand that? I think it's called peer pressure or something."

"I understand," Alison nodded. "But I'd like to see you race your car at a drag strip – where it's legal. If you promise me you'll do that, I'll accept this one time."

"And we can have dinner? Alone?" Denny smiled.

"Yes, we can," Alison nodded. "I like Italian food. And I don't mean Guido's Pizzeria. Remember that!"

Okay, I will!" Denny answered.

Alison stood from her stool and kissed Denny on the cheek. Denny reeled from the combination of the kiss and the fresh scent of Alison's hair. He nodded goodbye as he swooned in his seat; his angel had just kissed him and he was in 7th heaven.

"I've got to win tonight, no matter what!" he said aloud as he finished his jelly donut.

Chapter 17

Ground Pounders: Day of Reckoning

Tucker, Dawn, Hoyt and Bernice emerged from Big Boy's to see a crowd gathered around Tucker's '65 GTO. While the partial tubbing of the GTO's wheel wells was supposed to be a secret, some of the gearheads had not let it slip past them. Guys were crawling underneath the rear bumper, while others were under the front bumper – checking out Hoyt's home-brewed air dam.

"This Goat is rad!" said a bearded hippie wearing a huge peace sign medallion.

"Thanks," answered Tucker. "But this guy over here deserves all the credit."

The hippie turned to Hoyt.

"I might look like a lazy, pot-smoking hippie," he laughed, "but I own a chain of head shops and hip clothing stores. I'd like you to do some work on my '70 Chevelle SS and I also have a '64 Impala 409 that could use a little more juice."

"I'd love to," Hoyt grinned.

"If you guys win tonight, I've got a lotta friends with cars – if ya know what I mean," the hippie chuckled.

Tucker dug a business card out of his wallet.

"We'd love to service your cars, sir," Tucker said.

"We'll see after tonight," the hippie laughed. "I've heard about this Rager character and his protégé. I drove down here from Mackinaw City just to see this match up!"

"Mackinaw? Are you kidding?" Hoyt asked.

"Nope. They say you Woodward boys will become legends someday," the hippie nodded.

"No, no," said Hoyt. "That'll never happen in a million years. We're just young guns looking for some fun on the streets."

"Right!" Tucker agreed.

The Big Boy's parking lot was now filled to capacity and spilling over into the businesses on either side. The big race was just hours away.

Across from Big Boy's, none of the festivities were going unnoticed by Sgt. Harlan Boggs.

* * * * * * * *

Denny Stark arrived at Big Boy's a little late. He'd been cruising the strip for Alison's blue Pinto – or the LTD she had been driving – but she was nowhere to be found,

Denny thought she may have been so against this race that she'd opted out and was doing something else. He also prayed that Alison wouldn't arrive in Rager's Boss 429.

The busy parking lot of people abruptly opened up as Kent Rager's black beauty arrived with the plum crazy purple Challenger R/T in tow.

Rager pulled to the center of the lot and, as customary, stood on his doorsill. He waited until the majority of the crowd had gathered.

"It all comes down to tonight," Rager announced. "My young study and I are prepared to assume our place as Woodward Avenue royalty!"

The crowd cheered loudly, yet Rager was taken aback by the mix of boos coming from the gathered mass.

"Those of you who choose to boo me will soon change sides when you witness the two buffoons who have foolishly challenged us!" Rager yelled. "They are charlatans! And their little boy mechanic has wasted your time and money by claiming to be an ace mechanic, when all he really can do is bolt on a new intake manifold!!"

The crowd booed loudly, which was not lost on Hoyt, who was hiding with Tucker, Dawn and Bernice at a picnic table beneath a nearby tree.

"Don't let him get to you, buddy," Tucker assured Hoyt.

"Be sure to stop by for the bonfire when I burn that ugly orange Roadrunner to the ground!" Rager laughed. "And the GTO that I defeat will be chopped and sold for parts, so it can never haunt these streets again!"

"Oh boy!" Tucker laughed. "This guy is as crazy as he is evil."

"We're all aware of the atrocities performed by those heroes in Vietnam!" Rager bellowed out. "Well, our GTO driver was among those who chose to burn villages to the ground and toss hand grenades into bunkers filled with women and children!"

Tucker had heard enough. He stood atop the picnic table and called Rager out.

"Hey!" Tucker yelled loudly. "That foolish street thug has no idea what he's talking about!"

The stunned crowd turned to him.

"Yes, I was in Vietnam and yes, but never once did I, nor any of my brothers-in-arms, kill any women or children!"

"This baby killer is only lying to save face," Rager laughed loudly.

"Wrong again, Rager!" Tucker shot back. "Everyone here knows you're just a common hoodlum! You add nothing to this community. You're just a parasite on society!"

This did not sit well with Rager… at all. His face turned a bright shade of red and his hands were noticeably shaking.

"Let's settle this on the street, War Hero!" Rager screamed. "The gauntlet has been thrown down! Let your money and your worthless clumps of steel do the talking. It's time!"

The crowd erupted in uproarious cheering and applause. The throng headed for their cars just as Denny arrived to meet Tucker and Hoyt.

"This is it?" he asked.

"This is it, Denny," Dawn answered. "Best of luck!"

Denny climbed atop of the picnic table to take one last look for Alison's car, but was disappointed to see she wasn't there.

"This is it," he whispered to himself.

Secreted amongst the used cars in a lot across from Big Boy's, Harlan Boggs watched as dozens of cars exited the parking lot headed north on Woodward Avenue.

Boggs would be out of his jurisdiction, but had received permission from the Rochester police department to follow the action. He'd be assisted by the local law enforcement officers if he called on their radio frequency. When the last car was gone from Big Boy's, he slowly maneuvered his squad car onto Woodward Avenue.

Chapter 18

Ground Pounders: Don't Win… or Die trying

The hordes of cars swung left and right onto a long strip of country road just off Adams Road north of Rochester. The crowd lined either side of the road and waited for the arrival of the four cars that would fight for Woodward Avenue supremacy.

Denny was first to arrive in his beefed-up Roadrunner. The crowd's tone changed to a loud murmur as the Roadrunner's exhaust note created a clamor. Denny shut the car down at the starting line. He and Luke Fisher would be the first to compete.

Moments later, Luke's Challenger R/T rumbled to the line. Luke exited the car and was noticeably shaken. His cocky demeanor had been stifled by the size of his audience. He shuddered to think of hundreds of people mocking him if he was to lose the race.

Rager was next to arrive. He pulled his Boss 429 Mustang in behind Denny's Roadrunner. For some superstitious reason, Rager always chose the left lane.

Denny was surprised to see Stan and Ralph arriving in Ralph's worn down and dirty '66 Chevelle SS. He felt a deep concern as the two morons exited the red Chevrolet.

Lastly, Tucker arrived with Dawn riding shotgun. Behind them, Hoyt parked his Duster 340 on the side of the road. He immediately popped Denny's hood for some minor adjustments to the timing.

It was time for Rager to grandstand one more time as Stan and Ralph collected wagers from the crowd. He stood atop his doorsill again and addressed the crowd.

"Welcome to the big one!" he bragged. "This is a competition for pink slips and several hundred in cash to determine who reigns supreme on Woodward Avenue! Be sure to bet on the right cars and – by the way – the right cars are the goofy grape Challenger and my stallion: this beautiful 1970 Ford Mustang Boss 429! So place your bets!"

The crowd cheered and quickly surrounded Stan and Ralph, waving bills in the air.

"This is a half-mile extravaganza!" Rager hollered. "Don't miss out on betting on the sure winners!"

Hoyt closed the hood to the Roadrunner and gave Denny a wink.

"As long as you don't miss a shift, you're a winner!" Hoyt grinned.

Denny flashed him a thumbs up and a worried smile.

Luke's nerves were shot. He was a 17-year old high school student who had bitten off more than he could chew.

The cars sparked their ignitions and the combined rumble of exhaust would have brought a tears to the eye of even the most seasoned NHRA crew members. Each car revved up and left volumes of thick white tire smoke as they tacked-up their rear tires.

Stan hobbled to the line with a flashlight. He turned quickly and failed to turn on the light.

"Quit screwing around, you moron!" Rager yelled at Stan.

Stan turned his back again, checked the flashlight and turned quickly toward the two cars. The cars roared louder than Eddie Van Halen scraping his guitar strings at a football stadium concert.

The lighter Challenger had the advantage as they left the line and as quickly as they did, both drivers slammed second gear. Luke felt an adrenaline rush pumping through his veins, as he couldn't see the Roadrunner next to him.

But Denny was only recuperating from some tires slippage back at the starting line. The obscene amount of torque had broken his tacky rubber free of the road and his first 20 feet were spent spinning his tires.

Luke watched his side view mirror as Denny's Mopar approached. He was gaining ground, but Luke was about to blast off into 3rd gear.

Denny waited through 2nd gear for his tachometer to reach redline before he jammed the pistol grip into 3rd gear. The torque blew his head against the headrest and vaulted the Roadrunner just a half fender length behind Luke.

Luke was now giddy with adrenaline as he prepared to make the final shift into 4th gear. Denny realized he was not going to gain anymore ground! He jammed his pedal hard into the floor, hoping just a tiny bit of fuel would propel him beyond the Challenger.

Luke made a smooth shift into 4th gear and the Challenger sailed past the half-mile marker just a half-length in front of Denny's Roadrunner.

"Damn, damn, damn!" Denny screamed. He could've sworn he heard Luke's laughter coming from the Challenger.

"Haaaaaaa-ha!" Luke yelled and pumped his fist as he slowed the Challenger to the side of the road.

The cars turned and traversed back to the starting line with Luke waving to the cheering crowd. He stopped to give a high five to Rager who was especially happy. It was the first time Luke had ever seen Rager smile.

Tucker was concerned with Denny's loss, but for now, he had his own race to run. He climbed into his GTO and fired-up the 428 mill. The crowd began to turn their attention from Luke as they saw the GTO approaching the start line.

Rager sparked his Boss 429 to life and also crept to the line. Stan hobbled back in front of them and pointed at each car.

The Mustang and GTO both erupted in a glorious display of horsepower and billowing white tire smoke. The crowd went absolutely wild at the spectacle.

Backing to the line, both drivers revved their engines in anticipation of Stan's starting light.

Stan turned and shined the light.

Both cars leaped from the starting line with plenty of air under their front tires and within a matter of seconds, both drivers banged 2nd gear without incident.

Rager looked beside his car to see that Tucker's GTO was dead even with him. He kept his hand on the shifter and slammed it forward into 3rd.

Tucker shifted at the exact same time, but his Pontiac torque monster was had far more pulling power, which vaulted the GTO ahead of the Mustang by a fender length.

"Oh no you don't!" yelled Rager as he prepared to pull back into 4th gear.

Tucker knew Rager would be shifting soon, but he decided to hold it in 3rd gear for a few more RPMs. Rager banged 4th smoothly and as expected, his Mustang jumped to the lead by a half-length.

Tucker was hedging his bet that a later shift would propel him even with Rager before the half-mile mark and he wasn't disappointed; the GTO bounded forward and slightly ahead of Rager.

Now it was a race to the finish based purely on the horsepower at hand. Rager crept slowly even with Tucker and was gaining ground when he heard a sudden THUD! And with the finish line only 50 yards off, the GTO moved away and ahead of the Mustang as they crossed the line.

"No! No! No!" Rager screamed as he punched his headliner.

Smoke billowed out from under Rager's hood as he turned and headed back to the waiting throng of cheering spectators. Knowing Rager's temper, Tucker played it cool and quietly drove back to the starting line. As Tucker arrived, he was surrounded by a mob of cheering fans who either loved GTOs or had placed some major cash down on his victory.

Tucker exited the GTO and stood on the doorsill, waving to the dozens who surrounded him. Nearby, Denny was sulking against his Roadrunner.

"I guess this is goodbye, girl," Denny said at the verge of tears.

Denny had saved his money for years in order to pay cash for his Roadrunner. He lamented his foolishness in entering a pinks race against Luke and for ignoring Alison's pleas to back out.

Tucker, Hoyt and Dawn approached Rager, who was leaning against his Mustang.

"I think we should have a rematch next week," Rager said quietly. "I blew a rod or something."

The surrounding crowd booed Rager loudly at his feeble attempt to save his car.

"You can just hand over that pink slip and this ordeal will be over for you, Rager!" Tucker ordered.

Rager pulled his car's title from an inside pocket of his leather coat. He examined it and placed it on the hood.
Suddenly, Ralph stood between Tucker and Rager.

"This car ain't goin' nowhere!" Ralph yelled at the crowd. "He blew a rod! That means a rematch!"

"That's not how it works, Ralph," Hoyt said. "You guys lost – fair and square."

"Didn't I warn you about this, you little cockroach?" Ralph screamed at Hoyt.

"I chose not to head your warning, Ralph," Hoyt grinned.

"I should blacken your other eye then! Ralph bellowed.

Ralph reached beneath his shirt and pulled out his gun. The crowd began to retreat as he waved it in the air.

"Everyone back-off!" Stan yelled as he stood beside Ralph. Stan too, was holding a revolver and pointing it at the crowd.

"This Mustang is leaving and you can't do nothing' about that!" Ralph yelled.

Frozen in place, Tucker, Hoyt and Dawn didn't know how to react.

"Look. We can settle this like gentlemen," Tucker said as he held both hands up in front of him. "There's no need for violence. We made a bet and we won the bet Ralph. Even your boss pulled out his title."

Rager lit up a Lucky Strike and leaned against the Mustang. He was trying to remain neutral in this argument.

"The Mustang is ours now!" exclaimed Hoyt. "That was the bet!"

"Yeah?" Ralph spit onto the ground. "Well, here's your payoff, piss ant!

Ralph pulled the trigger and a shot fired off – the bullet piercing Hoyt's left arm. Hoyt fell to the ground as Dawn sprinted behind the GTO.

Hoyt squirmed on the ground. Holding his arm. "Did he just say *puissant*?

"No, it was piss ant!" Dawn called out from behind the GTO.

"Okay, thanks, Dawn," Hoyt called back as he writhed in pain.

In the meantime, Tucker stood his ground.

"You wanna shoot me too?" Tucker braved Ralph.

"Tucker! Don't!" Dawn yelled out.

Suddenly, Denny moved forward and stood next to Tucker.

"If you shoot him, you're going to have to shoot me too," Denny said calmly as he fixed a steely stare onto Ralph.

"You lost your damn car! You're outta this game!" Ralph said.

"But I didn't lose my friends," Denny said. "You shoot Tucker? You'd better be ready to shoot me before I tear your damn head off!"

"Oh, you're a real brave one, ain't ya?" Ralph laughed.

"What's it gonna be, Ralph?" Tucker asked again.

"Screw this!" screamed Stan, "I'll shoot the bastards!"

Stan stormed toward Tucker and Denny as the crowd screamed in terror.

Abruptly, as Stan raised his gun, shots rang out from behind the Mustang. Stan fell to the ground, his gun falling at Denny's feet. Ralph spun quickly and fired wildly before taking two shots into his chest.

Ralph collapsed forward into the dirt.

From behind the Mustang, Alison appeared, her gun trained on Rager. Harlan Boggs stood at the front of Rager's Mustang and covered Stan.

"What the Hell is this?" Rager yelled at Alison.

"Oh hi, Mr. Rager!" Alison smiled as she flashed a gold badge in his face. "I'm Sergeant Alison Chambers, Detroit Police Department... detective. Please turn around and place your hands on top of your car?"

Boggs holstered his gun and began cuffing Rager.

"Put him on the ground so he can't slither out of here, Sergeant Boggs," Alison said.

Alison checked Ralph's lifeless body and removed his gun. Tucker was keeping a foot on Stan's chest until someone could handcuff him.

"I'll get you for this, GTO man!" Stan cried out as he struggled to hold two gunshot wounds from bleeding out.

"Alison? What in the world?" Denny puzzled as he rubbed his eyes in disbelief.

"Oh come on, Denny," Alison laughed. "You've never heard of a female police detective before?"

"I thought you were a bank teller," Denny asked.

"Only when there's been a rash of bank robberies," Alison laughed. "I go where I'm needed."

"Damn," Denny whispered.

"By the way," Alison grinned, "I was very impressed how you stood up for Tucker. Maybe we can discuss that over dinner this weekend?"

Denny grinned from ear-to-ear.

Suddenly, Luke Fischer appeared. "I won your Roadrunner fair and square!" Luke yelled as he stomped his feet in the dirt. "A bet is a bet and I won that car!"

A voice in the crowd yelled out, "You didn't win a damn thing, young man!"

"Dad?"

The crowd parted as Dalton Fischer emerged from behind them.

"You're going home with me and I'm selling that damned purple nightmare!" Dalton yelled as the crowd erupted in cheers and laughter. "You're grounded for the next four years! No car, no trips and no extra anything! You're going to college and you'd better start getting your grades up or I'll shove a size 10 so far up your spoiled little ass you'll taste the leather!"

"Infantry?" Boggs smiled.

"Airborne!" Dalton exclaimed proudly.

Luke hung his head and walked over to his Challenger. He ran his hand over the car then reached in for his black leather jacket.

"You won't be needing that jacket, you little punk!" Dalton said as he ripped the coat from Luke's hands. Dalton looked around and tossed the coat to Hoyt who was sitting up on the ground as Dawn tended to his wounded arm. "I'm sorry you got shot, young fellow," said Dalton.

"No big deal," Hoyt grinned. "I'm alive!"

Alison pulled Rager to his feet, his hands cuffed behind him. When their eyes met, Rager smirked a menacing grin.

"So you banged me multiple times so you could make an arrest?" Rager grinned. "You're no better than a common street walker."

Alison leaned over Rager to whisper in his ear. "You've got it wrong, Kent. I "banged you" because I was falling for you," she whispered. "When the lies piled up, I could barely stand the sight of you."

Rager's grin faded away as he realized he'd lost Alison through his own evil lies and deeds.

"Detective Chambers, I want to thank you for protecting my son," said Dalton.

"It was nice to meet you," Alison answered.

CHAPTER 19

Epilogue

Tucker, Dawn and Hoyt were hosting their first-ever Christmas party inside the office at *Royal Oak Speed and Repair Service.* Tucker and Hoyt had given the grimy office its first major scrubbing since Tucker's dad, Alvin, opened the shop in 1947.

Denny Stark was there, with Alison attached to his arm. Steve Muller arrived with his wife and new baby – meaning that Muller's racing days were just about over for him. Tommy Clark had arrived with his '70 orbit orange Judge, despite the dusting of snow on the streets and Chip Brown kept checking the garage in order to look at his Hemi 'Cuda that Hoyt was rebuilding for him during the colder months. Bubba Baker arrived in his LS6 Chevelle.

Always the consummate nerds, Harold and Barry arrived in their latest version of a muscle car – a Ford Maverick Grabber.

"At least you guys are headed in the right direction this time," Hoyt teased.

Alvin and Edie Knox arrived just as the food came out. Alvin marveled at how bright his freshly cleaned office and restroom looked.

And Hoyt was no longer infatuated with Tucker's mom, Edie. Bernice arrived and made a beeline for Hoyt – hugging and kissing him until he blushed.

Sgt. Harlan Boggs and even Lenore from Big Boy's dropped by to share the holiday cheer.

Alison raised a glass and offered a toast.

"Ladies and gentlemen, a toast! I'm pleased to announce that Kent Rager was sentenced to 6 years in prison for grand theft auto," Alison revealed.

The small gathering cheered and applauded.

"Aaaand," Alison smiled. "Rager's thug, Stan Stanford was sentenced to 25 years in prison for the 2nd degree murder of Rick Irwin!"

Again, the friends all cheered.

"And finally," Alison winced a bit, "Lucas Fischer was accepted to U. of Michigan and will major in industrial design. Although he did have to surrender his driver's license for five years for street racing."

The small party booed the very mention of Luke, but most agreed that he was now on the right path. Tucker called out for another announcement and waited for the buzz to stop in the room.

"I have one more announcement to make," Tucker grinned. "Starting on January 1st, our good friend, Denny, will be working for the prestigious Royal Oak Speed and Repair Service!"

"Welcome, Denny!" Hoyt called out as the party applauded.

* * * * * * * *

Outside the speed shop party, Dirk Sturgis flipped a cigarette from his black Riviera as he peered through the front windows.

"You see that gang of turds inside there?" he asked. "Those are the dicks who tried to destroy my business. I'm lucky your brother kept his mouth shut and didn't try to plea out in court."

Sitting on the passenger side of Dirk's Buick, a dark figure leaned forward to take a look at the speed shop festivities.

"I've got this," he said as his chiseled features were highlighted by a drag from his cigarette. "My brother hired idiots. That was his downfall. My boys are smart attack dogs."

"Nice," grinned Dirk. "We'll get to work after the holidays."

"I'm in, Sturg."

And with that verbal agreement, 25-year old, Kurt Rager became Dick Sturgis' main supply pipeline.

TO BE CONTINUED....

Made in the USA
Monee, IL
28 November 2023

47646610R00127